THE FAIRYTALE KILLER

E&M INVESTIGATIONS | PREQUEL

LJ BOURNE

Copyright © 2020 by LJ Bourne

All rights reserved.

No part of this book may be reproduced in any form or by any electronic or mechanical means, including information storage and retrieval systems, without written permission from the author, except for the use of brief quotations in a book review.

ISBN: 9798392201198

1

I try to remember how I got here. But the icy cold spread all over my body in seconds. The last thing I promised myself before even the fuzzy, round lights of the world faded to black, was that I'd remember the way, that I'd fight unconsciousness and know where he took me.

Instead, I woke up lying on a thin, bumpy mattress, its twisted and bent coils poking me in the back and legs. My head is resting on a hard, thin pillow, which is already making the back of my head and neck ache. I've been here a while. The drugs are wearing off.

But I can't move.

My wrists and my ankles are tied to the edges of the bed, the bindings soft against my flesh, but unrelenting to my attempts at breaking free.

I see nothing either.

The blindfold is thick, wide, and soft, its edges tickling the bridge of my nose.

Smell and hearing are the only two senses left to me.

And they're not telling me much.

A faint scent of snow, pristine and deep, hangs over the room. I can smell the mildew and damp of the mattress and old sweat on the pillow, sour and nasty. The room itself smells of dust and wood. Not dirt, but I can tell the room hasn't been cleaned properly in a long time.

Another kind of smell grows thicker from time to time before fading away. It reminds me of raw meat.

The silence in my prison is so thick it's like a blanket over my head. I can hear the wind rattling against the window, making it chime, the way the messed up window in my apartment chimes. When that happens, the smell of snow intensifies and a freezing cold draft wafts over my bare legs and arms.

If I could get free of my restraints, I could escape out that broken window.

But I can barely move my arms more than a centimeter in each direction.

He called me Snow White.

And that's the only thing I remember clearly.

2

EVA

Three articles to finish, or I don't eat, but instead of writing, I'm staring out the uncurtained window behind my desk and open laptop, focused on the softly falling snowflakes, some as big as half my palm. And I'm not thinking about writing either. I'm thinking about what it'd be like to watch these same snowflakes leaning on Mark's wide chest, his arm wrapped loosely around me. Maybe we're sitting on a soft, fluffy rug in front of a roaring fireplace in some mountain cabin in the middle of nowhere, surrounded by soft snow and silence.

I curse, shake my head and look back down at the blinking cursor in the middle of a blank page. If I don't finish this article and mail it today, I'll be feeling the fat snowflakes falling directly on my head. Outside. In the cold. While I'm begging for change in Alexanderplatz, hoping some of the thousands of tourists there will take pity on me.

Lucky for me the article I've started working on today is a filler piece and I could write it with my eyes closed.

Tomorrow—today when this article will be published—it will be six months since the last of the princesses were found. Deathly pale, wearing gowns of silk, their eyes forever closed. Cinderella wearing a pink ball gown and one transparent plastic shoe, that was specific enough to give the police hope it will be traced easily, but wasn't.

Sleeping Beauty with her golden blonde hair neatly curled in the style of a Victoria's Secret model, wearing a translucent pale blue night gown, her hands neatly folded across her perky breasts and a glass tiara in her hair. She was found in the tallest tower of the American Church in Berlin, lying on the floor, but positioned exactly like the picture in the fairytale book my grandpa used to read to me when I was young.

In real life, Cinderella was Mona Florescu, who came to Berlin at seventeen from a village in Bulgaria to find a better life. By nineteen, she was working the streets. By twenty, she was immortalized as the first victim of the man who soon became known as The Fairytale Killer, the most twisted serial killer Europe has ever had.

Sleeping Beauty was Lara Dunholm, a Nordic beauty queen looking for a career in modeling. She came from Denmark when she was eighteen, trusted one too many false modeling agents, ending up addicted to heroin, and working the streets as a prostitute of the lowest standing. Most often, she found clients among truckers at the big gas stations on the wide highways leading into Berlin. Not the night she disappeared though. No camera at any of the gas stations she frequented showed her that night. Another dead end. Another hopeful trail gone cold. No kiss would ever wake her.

Both were poisoned with a lethal dose of valerian and benzodiazepines. Both were bled until not a drop of blood remained in their veins. Both were raped after they died. No prince charming came to their rescue.

Instead of waiting for the next princess to show up dead, the police took matters into their own hands, by getting the prostitutes—all prostitutes off the streets and heavily policing the areas where they made their money. Cruel or not to take away their only means of survival, the murders stopped.

They also brought in all the experts far and wide to hunt down the savage man behind the killings. The man who took such perverse pleasure in taking young lives, while twisting the happy, gentle memory of everyone's beloved fairytales beyond recognition.

As always, when I get to this point in the story, I have to stop and get up to stretch. Get out of my own head until my thoughts are clear. This is the place where what this sick man is doing really hits home. He's shredding happy memories of not just my childhood fantasies, but also of sitting on my grandpa's lap, looking at the beautiful pictures of gorgeous princesses while he reads the story.

One of the outside experts they brought in was Mark. He's a Special Investigator for the Criminal Investigations Departement of the US Military, stationed in Berlin. He's something of a legend over there, having solved a number of high-profile cases involving US Military personnel. That's at least part of the reason the German police were so ready to allow him to help them search for this serial killer. Not that Mark brags about it, or even talks about his career as an investigator much. But I know about it because I did some digging into his resume before we started dating.

There was little evidence to tie these crimes to a US soldier stationed here, but still enough of them for the US Military to get involved. As Mark later told me, after we got to know each other very well while I followed the case for at least five international newspapers who wanted someone on the ground, in the heart of things, but had no money to send their own reporters.

Mark was brought in mainly, because no one, especially not the local press, could imagine one of their own countrymen capable of such savagery. Serial killers like this only emerged in America. Everyone knows that. So it followed that the American military, which keeps a large presence here had to somehow be involved.

I said as much in some of my articles, though not in quite such cynical terms.

The six-month break in the killings could well indicate a soldier is behind them. Someone who has now been sent elsewhere. Mark is worried about that. I have not mentioned that possibility in any of my articles. Mainly from loyalty to Mark and his willingness to share his thoughts on the matter with me off the record. But also because I don't want to cause panic in England and Italy and wherever else the US has their bases. Somewhere in the US, if nothing else.

It could also be that he's been locked up for some other crime and is safely behind bars for now.

That's the hopeful note I'll end this *six months later* filler article I'm writing.

It's hard to peel my eyes away from the window, though. Twilight has gathered into a twinkling early evening, the streetlamps come on, prompting me to make a wish, which I forget the instant the light causes everything to sparkle, the snowflakes, the windows, the open umbrellas, and car windows below my fourth-story windows.

I think I wished for the killings to stop for good.

But I also wished for Mark not to be late picking me up tonight. We're going to a new Afghanistani restaurant that I've been dying to try since it opened a month ago. Actually, I've been dying to gaze into his soft brown eyes, which I bet will sparkle just as magically as the street outside. He's been away, working on a new case for two weeks now. In Kosovo of all places, but he called early this morning, to tell me he's returning this afternoon if the weather holds.

It held, and I hope he was on one of the planes that made it out of Pristina Airport before the smoggy fog made them close it down again.

I make myself another cup of coffee and bring my laptop to the kitchen table, facing away from the window. I need to finish the article, therefore I don't need any more distractions. Or else, I'll be the one canceling our plans for tonight. And in the stage of fuzzy-eyed falling in love I'm currently in, I'd prefer to live out on the street before I let that happen. I don't remember the last time a guy caused this kind of fog in my brain. It might not have happened before in more than twenty years since I first noticed boys.

The doorbell rings at exactly eight-thirty and I do ask who it is, but buzz him in before he can say. Then I open my front door, my heart pounding as his footsteps echo in the cavernous halls of this old mansion converted into an apartment building where I rent an apartment. My heart's racing and my face is flushed and hot despite the cold. It's impossible to heat the hallway and staircase of this old, high-ceilinged building, mostly because the narrow and long radiators under the huge widows on each landing are more often than not cold for one reason or another. It's not much better with the radiators in my apartment.

He's barely winded as he finally reaches my floor—fourth and last. I don't actually remember ever being this excited waiting to see someone, and this happy when I finally do, though I'm sure it's happened before. Just not with any of the guys I date.

His smile is wide and open and makes his chocolate brown eyes shine amber in the dim orange light in the hallway. His slightly wavy, brown hair is combed very neatly today, and he had it cut while he was away.

"You're late," I chide while he approaches, smiling just as wide, hoping the little tears of joy forming in the outer corners of my eyes won't mess up my makeup. I've always been a do-your-makeup-in-five-minutes-or-less kind of girl, but I've been trying a lot harder for Mark. Not that he ever notices and not that he doesn't most often tell me I'm beautiful in the mornings when my hair's all messed up and my mascara smudged.

"I came as soon as I could," he says, still smiling. "Trust me, I wanted to be here as soon as I got off the plane this morning."

That's one thing I love about him. He gets my humor and he doesn't get offended at every little criticism, slight or not. What I meant is that we agreed to meet at seven, but he had something come up and had to postpone, which he told me ahead of time and apologized for.

"No matter," I say once he's finally standing close enough to touch. "At least this way, I had enough time to make myself pretty."

I tried hard. I'm wearing a tight, ankle-length black sweater dress, made of a cashmere and merino wool blend. It hugs where it's supposed to hug and is loose where it's supposed to hide things. It's also as thin as cotton, but warmer than fleece. I spent a fortune on it, but I couldn't not buy it after I tried it on. I'm not sure how well I'll be able to walk in the high-heeled, knee-high boots I'm also wearing, given that the sidewalks are probably wet and sludgy from those pretty, large snowflakes that fell all day, but just that sharp, edgy desire in his eyes as they rake over me will make it worth it.

"You always look good," he says.

He's carrying a plain navy blue gift bag in one hand, but wraps the other around my waist, pulls me closer, and leans down to kiss me. That's another thing I love about him. He takes what he wants, when he wants and doesn't waste time on awkwardness or self-consciousness, or any of the other uncomfortable little things that make new, budding relationships so tedious. And what's even better, I know he'd look at me just as lustfully and kiss me just as deeply even if I was still wearing my sweats and the long thick woolen cardigan I never take off during the winter months, with my hair in a messy bun and no makeup, which is how I spent the whole day.

"I brought you gifts," he says, handing me the blue bag, as he leads me back into my apartment, his hand still resting on my lower back. Even with my highest heels on, he's still half a head taller than me and since the very first time we kissed, I've had the distinct feeling that I'll never be alone now that he's here to watch my back. Which is nonsense, since I love being alone. I think better when I'm alone. But that's another thing. I think very well when I'm with him too.

"Gifts as in more than one?" I ask, taking the bag and carrying it to the kitchen table where the light is better.

I pull out the bottle first, obviously. "Ooo, Rakia. How did you know?"

He shrugs, grinning at me as he leans on the arched doorway that leads from the hall to the kitchen. "Because you told me."

"And baklava," I say, the excitement in my voice not even a little bit faked. "The kind with pistachios. The best kind!"

It's not like you can't get baklava in Berlin, but it's just not the same as the true, back-home kind.

"I'll have to take your word on that," he says, peeling off the wall and walking closer. "I really dislike pistachios."

"That's perfect. It leaves more for me," I say and wrap my arm around his waist. "Thank you."

That's another thing. His gifts are never roses or stuffed animals, or pretentious bottles of champagne or wine, both of which I dislike. It's always something he knows I'll like because I mentioned it in passing. One of the first things he ever gifted me was a set of those sinfully expensive pens that I always lust over, but never buy because I can't justify the expense since I do all of my writing on my laptop and cheaper pens do the job just fine. He hears, notices, and remembers everything. And that's why I completely believe him when he says the things he says.

That and the kisses. Those are perfect too. I could spend the entire night just kissing him.

And we very nearly do.

3

MARK

As always, I vow to change the annoying, shrill, loud, and perky ringtone on my phone that wakes me. But before I even find my phone out in the cold living room of Eva's apartment, in my pants pocket where I left it last night, I know I won't, since I'm not sure any of the other ones would wake me so efficiently from a deep sleep.

"Good morning," the man on the other side says in hurried German before I even fully answer the phone. "Come to the Alexanderplatz police station as soon as you can. A car is waiting for you."

"What for?" I ask, not clearing my throat before I spoke, so my voice is all hoarse and raspy.

"It's happened again," the man says.

I don't even have to ask what, because I already know. The curt, panicked voice of the man who called

—Detective Schmitt—and the early hour can only mean one thing. The Fairytale Killer is back. And I'm supposed to stay away from the case. But I'm not even considering following that order. I've come a long way since this madman struck for the first time, and by the time I'm done, I might no longer be working as the US Military's Special Investigator. I might not even be a soldier anymore.

The sky outside the large wraparound windows of Eva's living room is a silvery blue. Not true dawn, but the cold morning light is not far off. At least it stopped snowing during the night.

"I thought you had the day off today," Eva says sleepily from somewhere behind my back.

I turn to see her standing in the doorway, her short blonde hair a messy halo around her pretty face. She's wrapped in that long, shapeless grey, blue and lavender cardigan she wears instead of a robe at home. It's swirling colors and how comfortable it looks always puts me in mind of long, peaceful days in a warm, cozy cabin somewhere far away from cities and murderers and death.

"I did," I say and walk to her, wrapping my arms around her. The wool is scratchy against my bare chest, but she's soft underneath it. This could be the last time in a long time I'll feel good. Gotta cherish the little things. I never appreciated how much that actually means until I met Eva. "But I have to go anyway."

"Is it him?" she asks in a shaky voice. "Today is exactly six months since the last one."

I look into her eyes, still dark because there's not enough light to show me the brilliant blue color they actually are. Like the sea in spring.

"It looks that way," I say. "Don't print it."

Her eyes narrow like I've offended her by asking her that. "You know I won't," she says defensively.

And I do.

I took a risk when I started dating Eva. We met while she was a reporter covering the first of the killings, always hanging around looking for tidbits to print. Reporters are cagy and full of tricks. They're like vultures circling a story and most of them would do anything to get it. But I trusted myself not to tell Eva anything about the case, since I never discuss the cases I'm working on with anyone. I work best alone. When she asked me for coffee one afternoon, waiting for me in front of the police station, I knew she wanted to probe me for information about the dead girl in an ancient ball gown found on the steps of Alte Nationalgalerie, or Old National Gallery, wearing just one transparent shoe. But I said yes to coffee with Eva anyway, because I couldn't look away from her lively, brilliant blue eyes after thinking about the dead girl's ice blue ones for three days straight.

I think even she was surprised when we ended up talking about everything but the case for six hours straight—all through coffee and then dinner and a drink after.

I was surprised when I could tell her about the case later. Somehow she understood my thoughts and conjectures better than I did myself as I laid them out. And she never put any of the things I told her in any of her articles. Not unless I expressly told her she could.

Now her eyes are sparkling at me, like bright high noon sun hitting the ocean, and I think we're on the verge of an argument. She's not a morning person and she doesn't like to have her integrity questioned. I learned both those things after our second date.

"I know you won't," I say.

"Good, you should," she counters edgily. "And I thought you weren't working the case anymore."

"I hoped so," I say. She's right in that I'm not authorized to go see the crime scene or whatever it is that Schmitt wants me to see. I'm going because I have to. It has nothing to do with being allowed to. Even I don't fully understand it. Yet, I do. The madman behind these killings needs to be stopped. The more people trying to stop him, the better. I'm one of those people.

I kiss her instead of trying to explain all that. I will, once we have more time, and I'm sure she'll be able to make better sense of it all than I can on my own.

Her eyes are soft and sleepy again once I pull away from the kiss to get ready, my blood flowing hotter and my mind clearer, for having kissed her first.

But my blood turns cold again before I reach the police station, and my brain is a frozen wasteland of purpose and determination. The razor-sharp, icy wind of early morning has nothing to do with it.

THE FAIRYTALE KILLER

It might've stopped snowing in the night, but the wind off the northern plains is vicious. The street is dark and empty, forbidding even, new buildings interspersed with the rubble left untouched since the end of WWII. It's only a fifteen-minute walk from Eva's place to the Alexanderplatz police station, but it feels like hours lost in some bleak nightmare. Bleak. This city's got all the reasons to seem that way going back decades, but somehow the prevalent vibe it gives off is hope and rebirth. Then The Fairytale Killer struck and changed all that. Now all the bleak and depressing cracks are showing.

I thought to get some breakfast and a cup of coffee on the way, but by the time I reached the first open coffee shop, my appetite was gone, taken by the bleak inevitability of the horror starting up again. The horror I, and everyone else in this city, hoped had gone to sleep just like the "princesses". Gone to sleep, never to wake.

The city's main police station is an imposing rectangular building, built with function not aesthetics in mind. A lot of this city was rebuilt that way, until old buildings and churches coexist with the utilitarian structures, rubble, and the ultramodern. A messy mix of everything coexisting side by side. Poor, rich. Utilitarian, historic. Communist, capitalist. All the extremes in such a small place. And now The Fairytale Killer. A serial killer with such a twisted mind, such degrees of sadistic enjoyment wrapped up in a methodical, well-planned package that all my training and all I've seen have not prepared me for it.

The Fairytale Killer in more ways than one. He not only stages his murders as scenes from the most famous fairytales but kills the wonder of them in the process. He's planned this for a long time. I understand that much about him. He takes perverse pleasure in making everything just so, just the way he wants it. I know that too. But much more than that, I can't be certain of.

"Inspector Novak, over here," a man calls to me just as I'm about to mount the stairs to the police station.

He's standing by a police cruiser. Hatless and jacketless, his cheeks quickly reddening from the biting gusts of wind. I think he's the one who puked at Cinderella's crime scene. Hans something.

"Where are we going?" as I open the passenger door to get in, ignoring him as he opens the back door for me.

"A forest near Eberswalde. It's about 50 kilometers out," he says as he gets behind the wheel.

I can barely feel my face, and I bet it's going to be much worse outside the city.

"That's near the Polish border, right?" I ask. It's an area I haven't explored yet.

The man nods and I settle back for the long ride.

As soon as we clear the city, the countryside stretches out flat and vast. Endless possibility it looked like when I decided to make my home here almost three years ago. But now the horizon is hidden in dawn grayness and some kind of fuzzy curtain that's probably ice crystals kicked up by the gusting wind, and I have no idea what I was thinking. It just looks bleak and bleaker. And the farther into the grey nothingness we drive, the worse the hopelessness becomes. I wish I'd kept my phone on silent last night. I wish I was just now waking up in Eva's warm bed, with the prospect of spending the whole day with her before me. But even that happy thought gets sucked up by the grey nothingness where it evaporates on contact. Like it never was.

Hans signals and turns off the highway. We're approaching blinking lights of blue and orange and white and yellow that light up the sky like a carnival. There's no less than three ambulances, six police cruisers, two fire trucks, a few crime tech vans, and five unmarked, dark sedans parked in an area maybe ten square meters at the edge of a forest. What did they find? An entire cast of characters from a fairytale dead and posed in the woods? I wouldn't put it past this monster we're hunting.

The lights were dazzling from a distance and they're blinding up close. Hans stops the car directly behind the last of the cruisers. The ground is so trampled that grass and rock are showing in places beneath the blanket of snow.

What the hell? Did the Germans suddenly forget

how to be careful and methodical in securing a crime scene? This bastard leaves so few clues as it is, why help him by destroying the ones he does by shoddy forensic work?

All the cars are still full of people though, their pale faces all fixed on me as I exit the cruiser. A vicious gust of wind hits me square in the face, making me wish I hadn't forgotten my scarf and hat before going to Eva's last night. But she makes me forget a lot of things and she makes most mundane things inconsequential. It's why I enjoy spending so much time with her.

"Novak!" detective Schmitt calls. "It's this way."

He's standing at a narrow opening in the line of snow-covered pines about fifty paces beyond the first of the cars. He's my age, about thirty-five years old. A thin man, head, and shoulders shorter than me, his dark hair hidden by a sensible hat that covers his ears and forehead. His bushy mustache is sprinkled with specks of snow.

"Why so many people?" I ask as I approach. What I really want to be asking is, Why me? I spent the first four months of the past six interviewing every US Military person in the area I could get access to and some I, strictly speaking, couldn't. I came very close to a disciplinary hearing because of it. I didn't sleep, I hardly ate, and my new relationship with Eva was almost nipped in the bud because of it. But I concluded that no active member of the US Armed Forces was involved in these murders. I reported as much to Schmitt and his superiors. But here I am anyway, the knot in my stomach frozen along with every other part of me.

"We didn't know what we'd need," Schmitt explains. "So we brought everything."

"Walk in my footsteps," he adds as he turns to enter the forest.

Many people already had, since the trail he's leading me down is a narrow path of packed snow.

"A call came in that there was a fire at a cabin in the woods at about four AM. The fire department responded, trampled and flattened the only approach to the cabin wide enough for a car and found no fire," Schmitt explains as we walk. His sentences as curt and formal as I remember them. This guy hates incompetence more than anything else and if he's not careful that futile hatred will eat him alive before he's forty.

"They had no grounds to enter the house, since there was no trace of a fire, but at least someone had enough brains to contact the owner," Schmitt continues.

The silence is undisturbed this deep in the wood and his voice is muffled by all the snow and the thick pines surrounding us. The sensation is not much different from the one right before you drift off to sleep. Listening to a fairytale, perhaps. Only this one won't have a happy ending.

"The man took his sweet time getting here from Berlin," Schmitt says. "He's some hotshot CEO, not to be disturbed by mere mortals for just anything, which this was in his opinion, so he took his sweet time getting to the cabin. He's the one who found her. He's not so talkative anymore."

Schmitt was born on the wrong side of the wall. He worked hard and had to jump many hurdles to be where he is, and he's got no love for the privileged that often still look down their noses at him. His real last name is Pozlovski, but he changed to his grandmother's maiden name to avoid as much discrimination as he could as he rose through the ranks. The dissatisfaction frothing inside him, just below the surface of his curt propriety made him a suspect in my mind and I investigated him as much as I could, given all the red tape involved. But by that point, I was grasping at straws. Not that this entire case up until now hasn't been grasping at a bunch of straws that broke as soon as we touched them. Schmitt couldn't have carried Sleeping Beauty up all those steps to the top of the tower where she was found. She was over six feet tall and outweighed him.

"In there, top floor," Schmitt says in a slightly wheezy voice.

The trees sheltering our approach have opened up into an almost perfectly round clearing. A poorly kept cabin made of dark brown wood stands in the center, the shutters on the windows mostly ripped off, and the glass of the few small windows facing us broken. The left part of the steeple roof is caved in and the falling shingles have destroyed the entire left side of the porch railing.

"Hansel and Gretel?" I ask quietly.

He shakes his head. "Thankfully, no."

About twenty meters separate us from the path to the front porch and we walk them in silence. To the left of the house, a wide path through the trees is blocked by a black Land Rover, a police cruiser, and a white forensic van. A grey-haired man is sitting behind the wheel of the Land Rover, wrapped in a dark brown blanket, his dark eyes huge in his round face as he watches us approach the house. But I doubt he sees us.

"The Investigator is here!" Schmitt yells at the house, causing the two crime techs in full-body white jumpsuits under their thick down parkas to look at us sharply from the back of their van where they're fiddling with something I can't see. One of them walks over and hands me a pair of white plastic shoe covers and black latex gloves without saying anything. My bare hands are already so chaffed by the cold and wind it stings as I pull them on, but I'm glad for the sharp pain. My head already feels like it's crammed full of the snow all around us and I feel the beginnings of a cold headache starting along my forehead. I wish the crime techs would bring me a hat too.

I'm about to ask Schmitt what the hell we're waiting for, when a white jumpsuit clad crime tech clutching a camera comes out of the building, muttering something that's muffled by the thick scarf wrapped around her face to the point of being unintelligible.

"Go on in," Schmitt says. "The owner says the cabin is still structurally sound, but with that roof, I'm not so sure. The last thing we need is for the whole thing to cave in before we comb through it. So we're doing this one at a time."

The first of the three wooden steps leading up to the porch creaks so loudly I wait with bated breath for it to break, but it holds.

The inside of the cabin is barely warmer than the outside, the only real difference is that the thin wooden walls are blocking most of the wind, though the chilly air still has no trouble entering through the cracks. My breath comes out in thick white plumes.

The front door opens into a narrow hall. The steps to the top floor are right in front of me. The stairs run along the wall on one side and have a wooden banister, made of thick, dark brown two-inch thick boards. It's slanted sideways, as though someone who didn't quite fit forced his way up them anyway. I'm guessing the main room of the house is behind the wall the staircase hangs on and that the kitchen is at the back of the cabin. Or maybe the kitchen is…

I stop my train of thought and take the first step upstairs. I know what I'm doing. I don't want to see the body. Once I see the body, the nightmare will be real again. I'd fooled myself into thinking this case was over for me, all the while knowing there was no chance of it.

Despite the frozen state of everything, I can still smell the dust that's been accumulating in here for years, maybe decades, while the owners let it fall to ruin. A shame. It's a lovely spot. Secluded, peaceful, serene. Not anymore.

The trail of many covered feet leading from the top of the stairs to the room is unmistakable and I follow it blindly.

I have to bend a little so as not to hit my head on the low doorway leading into the room.

She's lying on the queen-size, heavy wooden bed that dominates the small room. All the other furniture in the room—the two nightstands and the narrow wardrobe, is made from the same wood. I'm guessing the red and blue striped bare mattress she's lying on is filled with actual horsehair. All old, all way past its prime.

Not the girl.

She'd barely reached her prime before she was cut down.

Her heart-shaped face is porcelain white, almost shining beneath the carefully combed black hair encircling it. The red ribbon in her hair shines. A straight cut fringe covers her forehead and the sides reach to the nape of her neck. Her cheeks are flushed. Her lips are bright red, parted slightly, matching the ribbon in her hair. A bright red apple with a single bite taken out of it is held loosely in her open palm that's resting by her side. Her other arm is draped across her stomach.

She's wearing a pale green shirt with short, ballooned sleeves traced with dark red. It's tucked into a long, coarse light brown skirt. She's posed as though she bit into the poisoned apple then took ill and collapsed on top of the bed.

Like a doll. Not breathing. Her skin is as white as the snow surrounding this cabin. Just like a doll of Snow White taken straight from the popular cartoon.

But she's no doll.

Her left forearm is covered by a black-inked tattoo of a single rose, its thorny stem extending down to her wrist. The blooming flower is as red as her lips, but the monster who bled her and raped her before posing her as the image that cuts right into your childhood and rips it to shreds tried to cover it with white powder. It's caked now, revealing the red bloom, marring this perfect picture, making it just the work of a psycho.

It helps me to see the woman she was, not this grotesque doll he made her into. It lets me make a silent promise that I'll stop this guy before he does it again to another down on her luck young girl who had to work to eat despite the danger. Who had no one and nothing to shelter her from the man who turned her into this mockery of Snow White, a beloved character of girls everywhere, young girls with innocent dreams of princes and a charmed life.

The frozen knot in my stomach is roiling inside me. It'll do me no good to hate the man I'm hunting. It'll just cloud my judgment and make me do rash things. But that ship has sailed. I hate this Fairytale Killer more than I've ever hated anything or anyone. Not that my promises are worth a damn. I've been ordered off the case, threatened with a dishonorable discharge if I don't remove myself from this investigation.

I move over to the window, maybe in an unconscious need to get some fresh air even though the air coming in through the broken window and the cracks in the walls is quite fresh enough. The translucent, lacy curtains on the window are drawn, but despite that, I can see the approach to the cabin perfectly. It's actually a wide lane, made wider by the fire truck obviously, judging by the broken pine branches trampled into the snow on either side of it. And it's not so far from the main road.

No wonder all those cars were parked where they were.

Brilliant!

Transport the girl here. Arrange her. Then call the fire department to cover your tracks.

In the distance, where the lane joins the road, a pair of forensic technicians are examining the wide lane, nearly invisible in their white jumpsuits. They'll find nothing. But they'll try as hard as they can.

From the corner of my eye, I catch a glint in the trees opposite the lane.

Did he fuck up?

Maybe he couldn't resist watching us as we struggled to find at least one, single tiny shred of evidence that he didn't intend us to find.

I run down the stairs, not even hearing the creaking. Or Schmitt's yells for me to stop as I wade through knee-high soft snow towards where I saw the glint. I'm panting by the time I reach the first line of trees where something glimmered for the split second it took for me to notice it, but despite it, I'm willing to keep running until I catch the bastard watching us.

I most likely only have my training and experience to thank for keeping a tiny window of clarity open amid my blind hatred. I notice it a split second before I trample right into it.

A ring of stuffed—rabbits, foxes, birds, even a doe, even a wolf are arranged in a circle, their glassy, dead eyes all staring up at the room where Snow White lies dead.

Eerily familiar. One more page from our collective childhood gone, destroyed, crumpled, and discarded. If I ever have a daughter—not likely at my age, but still—how am I ever going to read to her the story of Snow White having seen this? How will anyone?

These killings reach beyond the horror of ritualistic snuffing out of young lives into the collective consciousness of goodness and happiness of everyone it touches. And it touches everyone. Hits where it hurts the most. I sound like Eva in one of her articles, but she's not wrong.

How can we catch a man who enjoys his kills this much?

How do we catch a man who plans every little thing down to what clues we're allowed to find?

I'm on the verge of puking by the time Schmitt reaches me. For the first time in my twelve-year career, during which I've seen all manner of gruesome and horrific, I'm ready to quit if I have to look at another dead fairytale princess.

"What do you think you're doing?" Schmitt pants and wheezes at me, but his curt tone loses its bite before he gets to the end.

His dark eyes are wide, reflecting the meticulously arranged forest creatures, all as dead as the girl in the cabin.

"I thought I saw someone watching from the trees," I say. "But it was just this."

I turn my back on him and the house. Somehow it's easier looking at the source of his shock than the weirdness that caused it.

The snow the animals are arranged in is barely disturbed, and no human tracks are leading to it as far as I can see. Just tiny paw prints. The dedication and planning that took. Sick doesn't even begin to describe it.

"She talked to animals or something," Schmitt says distractedly. "Snow White, I mean. In the story."

I shrug my shoulders. "I think so."

Actually, I know so. But I'm not willing to go any further down this sick rabbit hole this man dug for us.

Schmitt calls for the crime techs waving them over.

"There's something by the road they want you to see," he says.

I look out over the clearing, at the cabin, the trees,

the white-clad tech walking this way, the curtained window of the room where the girl is sleeping forever. And shake my head.

"The only reason I'm here is that it's my day off," I say. "The official ruling of the Criminal Investigations Department of the US Military is that these murders are not in any way connected to any member of the US Armed Forces. They've ordered me to stay out of the investigation."

Schmitt's wide eyes are now fixed on mine. "What?" he manages to ask after a few false starts.

"Karl," I say, using his first name since the situation seems to demand it. "I want to catch this guy as much as you do. But until there's new evidence warranting my participation, my hands are tied."

"You could've said so before," he says, stepping aside to give the crime techs room to work.

"I should've," I say and start walking back towards the cabin. "I don't know what I was thinking."

But I do know.

I want to catch this guy.

I want to stop this guy.

Whoever he is.

So when I got Schmitt's call this morning I ignored the fact that my hands are actually completely tied and I don't have leave to be part of the investigation anymore. But in the cold light of dawn, in this clearing that might see light but won't see the sun for months yet, that fact is hard to ignore. Impossible, actually.

"I'll ask Hans to drive me back," I say to Schmitt

once we reach the start of the path we walked here on. "It's better for the investigation if everyone agrees I was never here."

My phone is buzzing in my pocket. Hopefully, it's Eva, but it's probably not. I'd rather not answer it.

4

EVA

After Mark left, I lay in bed watching the sky turn whiter and whiter. We'd have no sun today, just a white, diffused type of light, before it'll turn dark much too soon. But what else is new this time of year?

My phones stayed quiet. No beeping to tell me of a fresh development, no news breaking. Whatever Mark went to see at dawn has not become public knowledge yet. But I'm sure it will soon. News travels fast, even in a city of three and a half million. Especially news of a serial killer.

If this was any other case, any other story, I'd be up and making phone calls by now. But as soon as the door closed behind him this morning, I realized that I was glad this story was over. Only it clearly wasn't. We were all fools to think it would be. I'm sure of that now, and I don't want to be.

"I'm coming home now," he told me when I called him around ten, drinking my first cup of coffee of the day, still wearing just the scratchy cardigan.

I showered and washed my hair, dressed, and did my makeup before he arrived. I'm the one who's playing what we have as a run-of-the-mill new relationship, as though he was the guy bringing me stuffed toys and flowers and kissing and hugging me awkwardly with no connection to me, just to the idea of me. I've dated plenty of guys like that. More and more as I got older. I'm the one unable to truly accept that I might have finally found the one man that I can be truly myself with. The one I can be alone with. Because we're the same that way too. We're both lone wolves, yet somehow we clicked. Maybe it's just because we're actually from the same country—Slovenia—even though he was born in the US and I've been living abroad on and off since I was twelve years old. When conversing, we speak in a combination of Slovenian, English, and even German. His Slovenian is rusty, but it's great talking to someone in my native language. Most of my family is scattered all over the world too, my sister in Spain, my brother in New York City, and my parents currently living the easy life of retirement by the sea at their country house in Croatia. I don't speak to any of them as much as I should. I was twelve when my family moved first to NYC and then London because of my father's job. In three years, I'll have spent a quarter of a century away from my home country. Sometimes I don't even entirely consider it that anymore. I moved to Berlin almost six years ago now, because it's such a culture-friendly, laid-back, diverse, artistic—bohemian, actually—city. It reminds me of NYC in a lot of ways, but the way that city used to be before overzealous gentrification stole its soul. I'm afraid gentrification is already doing the same here, but I still love living here.

"Was it bad?" I asked as he walked up the stairs, no smile or desire in his eyes this time. Only the happiness of being home, which I'm not sure I'm not just imagining.

He shrugged, gave me a quick hug and quicker kiss on the cheek, and went to the living room.

It's been hours and I still haven't been able to get him to talk beyond answering my thinly veiled probing questions with short, non-answers.

I took my laptop to the kitchen to do some work because I was getting angry at his silence and I didn't want to be. It's just the way he is, it has nothing to do with me. He just needs time to think, and sometimes that means he doesn't talk. It's not personal. It's nothing to do with me. It doesn't mean we're not well-suited. After a while of repeating that to myself, I calmed down.

I'm still getting no messages, no alerts that a new body's been found by the time I can't ignore my hunger anymore. It's two and the bustling outside my window—cars honking, sirens blaring, people shouting—is reaching that midday crescendo as it does every day about this time, especially in winter. It's like the last burst of life before night descends and everything quiets down again. The wind today must be vicious, since every so often a gust hits my single-pane windows, making them rattle and chime.

"How about I make us some lunch?" I say, leaning in the arched doorway from the kitchen to the living room. This apartment only has arched doorways, no doors, except the one to the bathroom. I like the spacious openness, but not the cold that's impossible to shut out in winter.

He's been sitting on the sofa, looking out the large windows at nothing in particular, since all he can see there is the grey wall of a socialist-era office-building with windows so small the occupants must stand right next to the windows to be seen. More than half of the offices in the building are unused, and most have broken blinds drawn day and night.

He turns to me and grins. "How about we order in?"

It's one of the two answers I expected and I grin too, shrugging my shoulders. I would've preferred the other possible answer, the one where he says he'll cook. He's good at cooking, and I'm not. At all. The only three things I can reliably make from scratch are scrambled eggs, spaghetti Pomodoro and potato salad. Though I'm also very good at heating pre-prepared, frozen dishes in the microwave. But I've been learning. By watching him cook, mostly. He enjoys cooking and he's really good at it. So my freezer is currently stocked with chicken as well as fish sticks. A step in the right direction, I thought, when I picked up the packet of meat in preparation for his arrival back from Kosovo.

"That works too," I say and stride over to the cabinet by the front door where I keep my stack of takeout menus. If there was such a thing as a professional takeout orderer, I'm it. I even keep notes on which dish is best where.

"Chinese?" I ask. "Or maybe Greek?"

"Your choice," he says, and I decide to just take him at his word. Although a part of me is bristling at him being so damn disinterested in everything today. But it's just how he is. He's distracted. Sometimes, when I'm deep in a story, I barely remember to return his calls or string more than three words together when I do. Story time, he calls it and understands.

"Greek it is," I announce. We pore over the menus, and he's not as disinterested in what he wants to eat as he was about what to eat.

"So, you ready to talk now?" I ask as I sit down next to him on the sofa after calling in the order. A question like that will always sound edgy and confrontational, I tell myself as he looks at me sharply, it's just the nature of it.

"You haven't heard yet?" he asks.

I shake my head. "Nope, not a peep."

He nods thoughtfully, lacing his fingers together in his lap and leaning forward.

"I guess Schmitt is keeping a tight lid on this one," he says. "Good. Gives him more time to work in peace."

"Did you advise him to do that?" I ask. After they

found the second body, the press was alerted just a couple of hours afterward, in what Mark called a panicked, headless chicken attempt at getting leads from the public, that probably made things worse rather than better.

He shakes his head and looks down at his hands. "I rushed there to see when I shouldn't have, but then I managed to remove myself before I made the mess worse. I'm not part of the investigation anymore."

"Not even now that he's struck again?" I ask. "I assume it was the same. Or similar, I mean."

He nods. "Yes. Meticulous attention to detail, every little piece in its proper place. Bled from jugular and the wrists, the cut super-glued together with military precision."

"So all the same reasons why everyone thought it's connected with the US Military again," I muse.

"It's Snow White," he says after a slight pause, adding, "You'll find out soon enough," speaking more to himself than to me.

"And she's posed as the American cartoon version, as all the others were," he says. "By tomorrow all the papers and bloggers will be screaming it's an American behind this. But I doubt Thompson will let me work on it despite that. He'll just say we can weather some bad press easier if a US Military Special Investigator isn't involved in the investigation. I've been sitting here, trying to figure out a way to convince him he's wrong, but I can't think of anything."

A part of the reasoning there is that if a German

was perpetrating these killings, he would have plenty of German fairytales to choose from, so why is he staging the American versions? Because he's American, of course.

Thompson is Mark's boss at CID and from what he always said, a very reasonable man.

"He might change his mind now," I offer. "I mean, he took you off the case when he thought the murders had stopped."

"The order to stay away came from much higher up. As long as the US Military is investigating, it looks like we're tacitly accepting the blame. As some of your press friends have been so eager to keep pointing out," he says.

"Not me—" I interject.

He turns to me and smiles. "No, not you. And you can't print any of what I just told you either. Especially not the superglue thing."

"I know, and I'm not going to." I have to bite my lip to stop the indignation from welling up. The superglued cuts—the one clearest connection to the Military since that's how they triage wounds on battlefields—is something he told me awhile ago and I kept my word, I never printed it anywhere. But I'm not about to start an argument with him when I just got him talking again.

He flashes me a weary look from the corner of his eye but then focuses them on the jewel of communist architecture across the street from my apartment. Or maybe he's looking at the flat land beyond it. So full of possibility, I always thought. So full of nothingness, he seems to be thinking.

"What none of them understand is that I need to be on this case," he says. "None of the cases I've worked on before this one, and there's been a lot of them, ever got under my skin the way this one has."

He looks at me, and in his eyes a mixture of shame, regret, and well-hidden wild panic. I wrap my palm around his interlaced hands and use the other to caress his cheek. He doesn't shy away from what a lot of other men would construe as pity. It's caring. It's compassion. I don't feel sorry for him.

"I understand, Mark," I whisper. "But what the hell else are you going to do? Orders are orders, right?"

I wish I had better advice to give him. But from what he told me, he could be facing a discharge from the military if he doesn't step away from this case, and with everything else this Fairytale Killer has already taken, I don't want him to destroy Mark's career too.

He grins and narrows his eyes in ironic acceptance. "Yeah. Orders."

The doorbell rings just then, and while I'm waiting for the delivery guy by the door, Mark gets a phone call.

I didn't hear his side of the conversation, but he's paler than he had been all morning, his face hard like it was carved from ice when I reenter the living room carrying the plastic bags with the food.

"I have to go into the office," he tells me.

I could ask why, but he wouldn't tell me. His silent mode is back on.

"I'm sorry," he whispers as he kisses my cheek by the door, already wearing his coat and shoes.

"It's all right," I tell him. "Call me when you can."

He nods and leaves and I know he will. We've been together for six months—well, more like four, since he's been away working on cases around Europe for two of them—and there's no logical reason why I'm so sure of him, but I am.

5

MARK

The US military base, which also houses the CID is a huge, sprawling complex just outside Berlin city limits. It's seen its share of history over the years, but has, lately, become a bustling, vibrant sort of place as the army has started working on community outreach more and more. The severe, utilitarian narrow building that houses the central command, CID as well as several other departments, looms large over the smaller buildings housing the barracks, garages, mess halls, cinema, rec centers, and other necessary parts to a military base. This base, or Kasarne, as it's called in German, was fully equipped when we took it over decades ago, so it has that air of permanence and history—home, even—that so many other US Military bases, erected for the sole purpose of serving as such, do not.

I took a taxi from the city center but had the driver drop me off before we reached the gate in the tall concrete wall, that still has the metal rods that were used to attach vicious barbed wire to when this complex was a much more severe place. No barbed wire remains, and most of the rods are rusted nearly all the way through. One day they'll have to be removed too, but that lengthy and time-consuming project hasn't yet floated to the top of any to-do list.

I walked past the check-point and along the neatly paved path lined with two small groves of leafless trees that make the approach to the high command building seem like you're just visiting any old, run-of-the-mill place. The walls are still white for the most part, dotted with narrow, tiny, identical windows. One hundred of them, spanning four floors. I counted. The red double doors directly in the center of the building are the only entrance from this side and I'd much rather be standing outside marveling at the simplicity of the design of this building than going in to face anything but a simple summons.

The secretary who called me earlier just told me to report to Major-General Thompson right away and hung up as soon as I confirmed the message. Clean and efficient. But the torrent of thoughts and fears it unleashed in my mind was anything but.

The one thing I realized while wracking my brain all morning on how to get myself back to the case, was that I best cool off and take a step back. I'll tell Thompson as much, and I hope he'll listen. I don't think they can court-martial me for visiting the crime scene this morning, but who knows. Nothing about this damn case is normal.

"Come," Thompson says curtly from behind the cracked open, double-sided, gleaming oak doors as the secretary announces my arrival.

Followed by, "At ease," as I enter and salute him. "Sit."

I opt for one of the green leather chairs facing his wide, dark brown-wooden desk. Most of the offices in this building have been fitted with modern furniture over the years, but not Thompson's office. The floor is covered with a thick, dark red and blue Persian rug, the walls are lined with meticulously crafted cabinets of dark hardwood—oak, most likely, though I'm no expert—and they match the large desk that dominates the space. It's as neat as always, even despite the crumpled, stained envelope lying sideways in the center of it. His office chair is black leather, shining as though it was assembled just this morning, though it most likely had been occupied by a Nazi or two since it was actually new. As was the chair, I'm sitting in, I'm sure.

"You saw the body this morning," Thompson says. Not a question, not a statement, but something in between. There's no reason to deny it.

"Detective Schmitt called me and I went there, yes," I say. "But I took no part in the investigation."

Other than running like a madman through knee-high snow and messing up the already very little chance of getting a shred of evidence beyond what the madman wants us to find. I've been trying not to think about that part all morning.

"Snow White?" Thompson asks in a defeated sort of voice. It's not really a question, and that throws me for a full two seconds.

"How did you know?" I ask. "Did the Germans alert you?"

I find that hard to believe. I was the only go-between for the Germans and CID and I doubt that's changed since we have removed ourselves from the investigation.

He doesn't answer, so I continue. "Yes, it was Snow White. And her little forest animals. Same as the others. Planned and staged perfectly. I doubt they'll find anything. But I walked away. As per my orders."

It doesn't do to get snarky with your superior officers, and my tone isn't lost on Thompson. He looks at me sharply from beneath his bushy, dark brown eyebrows, which are speckled generously with grey. His short-cropped hair is thick too, but all grey. His dark eyes are always just sharp. It's impossible to know what he's thinking from looking at them.

"I'll let your insubordination this morning slide, Novak, because I'm rescinding my orders," he says. "I got a letter this morning."

My eyes snap to the manila envelope in front of him. What I thought was dirt is actually fingerprint dust. And it revealed nothing. No surprise there. The envelope is addressed to Thompson in a flowing script, written with a firm, certain hand in black ink. There's a stamp in the corner. A small denomination one. Local.

"Open it," Thompson says. "It's already been processed."

The nausea that almost unmanned me when I found Snow White's loyal forest creatures is threatening to do so again as I pull out the stack of photos from the envelope.

Pocahontas, leaning on her canoe in the tall grass by a lake.

Sleeping Beauty sitting by an old-fashioned spinning wheel, her dead eyes focused a single red drop of blood on the tip of her finger.

Cinderella in her rags, cleaning a dusty fireplace, a man holding a glass slipper for her to try on.

Snow White in her bed, a man in a white outfit, his back to the camera kneeling beside her bed, head bowed in defeat.

"What is this?" I ask, looking up at Thompson, really wishing he could tell me, give me some rational, logical explanation. Not tell me what I already know.

"This one," I say pointing at Snow White. "She's the one we found this morning. But there was no prince in white there."

The man in the photos is the same one, I'm sure of it. He has his back to the camera in both the photos, but it's the same wide back and big biceps in both. The angle is such that it's impossible to gauge his height since he's kneeling in both photos. Maybe the forensics department has something, anything, to make him easier to identify. But I doubt we're that lucky.

"But what are the others?" I mumble, even though I already suspect.

"We're reopening the case," Thompson says. "You're back on it. And Otto Blackman is flying in tonight to help."

I snap my head up from studying the envelope, which has no return address, and no postage stamp. It was hand-delivered to Thompson. And very few people have that kind of access.

"I can catch this guy," I say. "I will catch this guy."

He nods. "I know you will. But Otto was you before he retired fifteen years ago. He knows his stuff. And we need all hands on deck as our Navy brothers would say, if we're to catch this psychopath. Don't you think?"

Comparing Blackman to me is a huge compliment and completely undeserved. Colonel Blackman is a legend at CID. He's solved more cases than any other US Military CID Special Investigator and maintained a solve rate of almost ninety-nine percent during his twenty-year career.

I look back at the photos arranged on the desk in front of me. I don't even remember laying them out.

"Yes, Sir, you're right. And Blackman caught two serial killers in his career if I remember correctly. The Colorado Hoarder and the Bangkok Strangler."

Thompson nods. "Blackman is an expert on serial killers. He's been teaching all over the world for the last fifteen years. Some say he left because he was burned out, though that's not what he told me."

He pauses, a farseeing look in his eyes.

"You and he are friends?" I ask, not even sure why.

"Yes, he's coming in as a favor to me. We were at West Point together," he says, a half-smile on his lips like those were some great times he's remembering. "I've wanted to bring him in since this mess started, but he told me he left CID because he couldn't face another dead body or grieving relative. So I didn't ask him. But now, I think we need all the assets we can find."

I nod even though it wasn't really a question.

The young women in the photos, posed as beloved characters from age-old fairytales and cartoons, are most certainly dead. And apart from Snow White, they're not from any crime scene that we've found. Yet.

6

EVA

What started as an early morning bomb of nerves, apprehension and anxiety turned into an absolute whirlpool of the same by the time evening rolled around. Mark hadn't called, and he sent back a one-word text —*Later*—to my probing. The streetlights outside are twinkling in the moist winter air, people walking more leisurely, with more heart and purpose now that the grayness of day has turned into sparkling night. It's usually like that on late winter nights when everyone's absolutely fed up with the cloudiness and the cold.

I settle down with a glass of cold white wine, Pinot grigio, lately my favorite, and open the novel I started reading back in late autumn. It's by an up and coming literary talent, hailed far and wide, but to be honest, I have no idea what I'm reading. A book of the weirdest possible poetry would probably make more sense than this "story," but I need to get out of my own head for a while. Out of my life.

Every device connected to the internet I own starts chiming just as I make it through the first page of the convoluted prose. My two phones, my laptop, even the desktop computer in the corner of the living room I haven't really used in over a year. I didn't even know it was on.

I've expected something like this all day. Ever since Mark got that dawn phone call and left to look at a crime scene he then told me nothing about. But try as the police might to keep something like that a secret, the network of reporters that I'm a part of have their connections everywhere. I texted a couple of mine, but haven't heard back.

Now the internet is exploding.

I left both my phones by my laptop on the kitchen table when I finally gave up trying to work. The screens are covered by notifications—emails, Twitter and Facebook messages, breaking news articles from news agencies who report only the facts as they become available, blog posts by amateur sleuths. I scroll down the screen to find the first notification, but they just keep popping up, faster and faster.

What is this?

I open a text message at random, from Kosta, my Macedonian ex. The two of us work much better now as friends. "Did you see? A body was found by the

Havel river in Gatow. They're saying it's that Indian princess."

The next couple of messages show me fuzzy photos of the lakeshore, a canoe clearly visible, the long-haired woman in a light-colored leather dress not so much. Photos taken by gawkers and passersby. The bank of the Havel is a popular strolling spot, even in the clutches of winter.

Then I open a crisp photo of a woman in a blue dress, her long white-blonde hair neatly curled in luxurious waves held back from her face by a scarf of white lace. She's sitting in a straight-backed chair by a window, an old-style spinning wheel in front of her, a drop of red blood the only thing marring her porcelain skin. Sleeping Beauty at her spinning wheel.

A body was found in an unused cabin owned by a Berlin banker in the woods near Eberswalde. Sources say it's the work of the serial murderer known as The Fairytale Killer, but the authorities have not yet confirmed that, reads a short article by DPA, the German Press Agency.

My stomach is a knot of nausea so deep and hard I doubt I'll ever be rid of it by the time I'm staring at a picture of the peacefully sleeping Snow White, wearing the exact same outfit I remember from the storybooks of my childhood. Uncanny. Something inside me lurches, as though I've lost my footing stepping from that happy time to this nightmare even though I'm standing perfectly still, holding my breath.

What is this?

But I know what it is.

Three new bodies. Three new deaths at the hand of The Fairytale Killer. Found in one day.

He didn't go away for six months. He wasn't arrested. He wasn't stopped.

He was planning this.

7

MARK

It's not common knowledge that the basement of the command building at the base also houses a state-of-the-art forensics lab, which is responsible for processing most of the evidence collected by the CID in Europe. Evidence that's connected to the investigation of our personnel, that is. Their services were made fully available to me while I helped Detective Schmitt and the rest of the locals investigate the first two murders. I stretched that clearance to the limit and aways beyond.

But if I hadn't, we probably still wouldn't have known that the superglue used to seal the victims' wounds is manufactured in a small factory in Kentucky that lost the cushy contract with the US Army fifteen years ago to a much larger corporation that also supplies our field kits, laces, belts and medical field kits issued to all personnel, as well as all the spoons, forks, knives and plates and a whole vast array of everyday items too numerous to list. Although that finding did point at the US Military initially, none of the old super glue could be found in any inventory logs in Europe or the US. A small stock of it remains in Asia, on record at least, because when I asked them to find the actual box, none of them could. I seriously debated catching a flight to Bangkok and finding the damn thing myself, but then I was told to remove myself from the investigation.

After they lost the contract, the Kentucky firm took their vast supply of the glue and sold it to be used as generic drugstore brands. Walmarts and Kmarts and who knows who else are now selling it nationwide at steep discounts.

My keycard won't open the stainless steel double doors on the corridor that leads to the lab. Knocking on it won't be heard by anyone, nor will calling out and banging is out of the question. Even in my agitated state, I know that. I'm fumbling with my phone, trying to find the number of the lab head, a Major Stanley, when the door opens on its own and the woman in question is standing in front of me. Her long, dark brown hair is securely fastened into a bun in the back of her head and her vibrant dark brown eyes are shooting fire even as she greets me quite properly.

"We were told to expect you, Sir," she tells me.

I almost got her discharged when I lied to her about having clearance to test Detective Schmitt's DNA against the sample from Cinderella's crime scene. The first Cinderella crime scene? But no, I won't start thinking about it that way until we're sure. It didn't match, and I didn't have the clearance. I was grasping at straws and I almost took a lot of people down with me. This time, I'm doing it by the book.

"Marisa will take care of your access codes. Give her your keycard," she says over her shoulder as she walks briskly to the other set of double doors at the end of the short corridor. This door opens into the main room of the crime lab. It's dominated by a large rectangular table, two meters long and one across. The table is higher than a regular table and can do many things, including project detailed maps, which is what half of it is being used for now. Sargent Ross, or simply Eager Ross as I like to think of him, and timid Wanda are poring over it, their backs to me as I enter, so I can't see what they're looking at.

Ross, in his eagerness to help as much as he could on the case, revealed to my superiors all the interviews and evidence gathering I had him doing for which I technically didn't have the authorization, but which I figured were essential. These included everything from interviewing army personnel who had no clear connection to the case to using the Army's resources to trail Detective Schmitt for a couple of days. Ross helped me with a lot of this, not knowing it wasn't by the book. So I don't blame him, but he almost cost me my job when he reported to Thompson and got me taken off the case much too soon.

The wall over the table, across from the door is covered by a large screen which can also be used for a number of things, but right now it's showing the blown-up images of the five photos Thomason received and which I'm clutching in the envelope in my right hand. The table and the screen are controlled by the wall of computers behind which I can just make out a part of Marisa's cornrowed head. She's in charge of intelligence gathering and everything related to computer work, and she's amazing at what she does, and I'm truly very sorry she also got caught up in my ill-advised investigation of Detective Schmitt.

The lab has over fifty full-time staff, but the team I worked closely with for the last two murders are all in this room. The others, probably working in evidence rooms behind the closed steel doors lining the left side of the room, I met only in passing, some not at all. The right side has the four glass-walled cubicle offices, the largest Marisa's lab room, the next largest Stanley's office, and the third and fourth shared by all the rest.

None of them seem particularly overjoyed to see me.

"What have you found so far?" I ask, opting not to make any apologies for the fact that I'm here again, or any promises that I won't jeopardize their careers again. I already made those apologies and I mean to take better care from here on in, but I also mean to catch this madman. Now more than ever.

They all fidget, glancing from one to the other, mostly at Stanley. She clears her throat.

"No prints on the envelope or the photos, no DNA either. We're looking into the origin of the envelope, but it looks to be a standard type that can be purchased at any post office or stationery store," Stanley explains. "Seeing as only one of the crime scenes depicted in the photos have been discovered so far, Ross and Wanda are working off the photos to try and pinpoint the most likely locations of the others."

"And there was a single, long strand of hair in the envelope with the photos. Light blonde, not dyed," a man says behind my back. Major Wyatt, the DNA tech. "Unmistakably female. We're waiting for DNA and then I'll run it against the victims. And I assume the Germans will want to run it against their databases as well. You'll be the contact point for that?"

Full cooperation with the local authorities, those were Thompson's orders when I first started working on this case. If it's one of ours behind these sadistic killings, we will not shelter him, were his exact words. The man is nothing but just and fair. Which is why I couldn't quite understand the vehemence with which he wanted me off and away from the case two months ago.

"Yes," I say. "The Major-General has given me the necessary clearance."

A single strand of female hair. Seemingly the perfect clue, but I bet it's just going to be another wild goose chase. Like the transparent shoe and the diamond ring on Sleeping Beauty's finger. Both looked like they could break the case. Both were monumental dead ends.

"Any luck on pinpointing the locations?" I ask as I walk over to Ross and Wanda, making eager Ross turn to me sharply and timid Wanda shiver.

"We've been focusing on Pocahontas," Ross explains hastily. "There's the most detail in it, we thought it'd be easiest, but there are so many canals and lakes and rivers around here and this kind of grass grows alongside at least a part of all of them."

They have the photo of Pocahontas blown up and attached to the table, with the interactive map of a lakeshore below it. It's touch operated and they've been scrolling along it trying to find the matching piece of shore.

"She rowed her canoe on the river, didn't she?" I ask, confronted now by the wide eyes of both Wanda and Ross.

I clear my throat. "In the cartoon, I mean?"

My mother was nineteen when she had me, and we watched and re-watched these princess cartoons long after I was no longer even slightly interested in them. She was, and it was something we did together. We did everything together while I was growing up. Now I speak to her once every three months, if that much. But this is not the time to be worrying about that.

They exchange a look. "We'll check, Sir."

On the other side of the table, the copies of the photos arranged one next to the other, the table dark under them. I walk there and fumble for the light switch to turn the backlight on. It comes on its own before I find it.

"These aren't digital photos, are they?" I ask.

Marisa walks to stand by my left shoulder, Stanley at the right.

"Well spotted, Sir," Marisa says. The inner city cockiness is still noticeable in her voice, however much she tries to hide it. "They're old-school, using film, and developed by hand."

"And the man? What can you tell me about him?" I ask.

She shakes her head. "I'm still running some algorithms to try and at least tell you how tall he might be standing, but even that won't be too accurate. He's out of focus in the photo. But I think this could be the edge of a neck tattoo," she points at a tiny black blob above the collar of the man's fancy white jacket. I peer at it closer, but all that does is make it fuzzier.

"That could very well be a dust speck on the lens or an imperfection in the photo paper," I mutter, not really sure why I spoke it aloud.

"You're right, Sir," Marisa says.

"Good work," I say anyway, and she nods curtly. "I'm guessing these are the originals?" I ask, pointing at the photos on the table. "And the envelope contains the copies?"

"Yes," Stanley says. "The envelope isn't a copy."

I take out the photos and hand the envelope to Stanley, then ask for a folder. Ross practically skips to bring me one from the communal office.

"I'll take these to Schmitt, see if he can make anything more of them," I say. "Keep me posted on all you find. However small."

They assure me they will and after Marisa arranges the necessary clearance on my keycard, I leave the lab.

I'm betting Schmitt had Snow White transferred to the Medical Examiner's office by now and is already breathing down the man's neck to speed the examination along. Who knows, maybe the Germans have already found some key piece of evidence that will break this case wide open. One can hope, right? Not that I am.

The day's grey-white light has turned to dusk while I was inside and the first gust of fresh air that hits me as I exit the command building is razor-sharp and biting, carrying all the frost it picked up in the far north where it came from. It feels like the first breath of fresh air I've taken in days, even though it's only been a couple of hours since I was outside. It's also a clear reminder that I need to pull myself together if I'm going to be any use to anyone in this case.

I call Detective Schmitt and the phone rings for an uncharacteristically long time. He's the type that answers every phone call right away, even in the middle of a conversation.

"Are you supposed to be calling?" he asks as he finally picks up just as I was about to hang up.

"Yes, I was cleared to continue investigating," I tell him. "Are you at the station? I have to show you something and then I'd like to see the body again."

"I'm at the bank of the Havel river in Gatow. Come quickly," he says. "You'll see the lights."

And before I can even fully react to his ominous words, the line goes dead. I'm clutching the photos much too tightly, crumpling them, most likely, and I force myself to relax my grip.

It's started. They found the first one. Pocahontas. There goes the hope that the photos are just an illusion, a hoax, fake. Not that I truly believed they were. I just hoped.

8

EVA

My other phone, the one I use only for business calls and communication with the various editors I work with, is ringing. That one hasn't been blowing up as much as my personal one.

"Hello, Christina," I answer absentmindedly. She's an editor for The Guardian now and commissions a lot of articles from me. We go way back, since we studied journalism together at the London School of Economics.

I keep scrolling through the images I got on my other phone, looking for the one that sparked something in my mind. Something I was supposed to pay attention to the first time I saw it and now my heart's pounding, anxiety making my head feel like it's full of bees buzzing nervously because I didn't.

"Hello? Eva? So, can you do it?" Christina says sharply, cutting through the buzzing in my ears.

"Do what?"

"Get me something on Snow White by four AM?" she says. "For tomorrow's print edition."

"I'm afraid I can get you more than just that," I say quietly.

I found the photo. It's of Sleeping Beauty poisoned by the prick on her finger. I know her.

"What are you talking about, Eva? Hello?" Christina says impatiently.

"I'll call you back," I mutter. "And you'll have your story, I promise."

Selima. That was her name. A twenty-five-old from Sarajevo.

Once it became known that The Fairytale Killer was choosing his victims from among the unregistered prostitutes working the streets of Berlin, I sought them out. A lot of them are from former Yugoslavian republics and I speak their language. It wasn't hard to get them talking. They were scared and alone and without options. Out of that came a piece I didn't intend to write—about the dark side of legalized prostitution, such as they employ in Germany, and about all the poor women it leaves behind, unnamed, unnumbered, uncared for. It ran in The Guardian originally, but it was picked up by most major European newspapers as well.

Selima wouldn't forgive me for writing the article, blamed me and the article for the police chasing them off the streets wherever they tried to earn a few Euros, as she put it. She wouldn't believe me when I told her it was to keep them safe from the psycho hunting them.

Maybe I'm wrong. Maybe it's not her. Those are my only two clear thoughts as I put on my boots, heavy down jacket that comes down almost to the ground, wrap an oversized shawl around my head, pocket the phone and leave the apartment.

Maybe I'll find her safe and sound. But none of the hopefulness of those jittery thoughts is reaching the cold, icy knot that's settled in my stomach. The one borne of knowing that I'll never speak to Selima again.

In Berlin, there are plenty of streets where unregistered prostitutes ply their trade, but only three are well known. All of them are deep on the former east side of the wall, and none of them is a good place to be. The first I visit is more an alleyway than a street, stretching just wide enough for a car to pass, and sandwiched between two long-abandoned tall buildings. One of them was a cloth factory built after World War II to supply most of the region with linens, shirts, and uniforms. The other was where the factory workers lived so they wouldn't have to walk far to get to work. The factory has stood abandoned since the 1970s, but the apartment building was rented out until the late 1980s when it finally fell into such disrepair even the poorest of the poor wouldn't pay to live there.

The apartments inside are quite spacious, and most of the units have either open fireplaces, masonry heaters, or both. A few of the Eastern Bloc girls I interviewed for my article on underground prostitution in Berlin, who had come illegally and didn't have much choice but to continue living illegally, made their homes in them. The fireplaces and heaters made it easier to stay warm during the winter, and the vacant rooms to entertain their customers in are in ample supply here. For years, the authorities looked the other way. Not so when my article revealed it all.

The alley is pitch dark at both ends, the only illumination coming from the single working streetlamp in the middle of it. My heart's thumping and my hands are shaking, but I'm not even considering turning back. As I enter the alley, a cold gust of wind catches my parka just right to send the cold air right under it, the down it's filled with offering no protection.

The long, narrow alley is deserted. Only trash is moving, dancing in the wind, and the few windows of the apartment building on the left-hand side are all dark, not even a slight orange candle flame flicker in any of them.

Selima had made herself a cozy home in one of the apartments in that building. She blamed me and my article for the raids that forced her to leave it. Clearly, she wasn't exaggerating about the police clearing this street of illegal prostitution. No one's lived here in months. Even the trash is grey and old, the signs on the packages flying around in the wind unreadable.

But maybe she is still here. Maybe she came back after the raids when things quieted down again. As I remember, she chose one of the bigger units on the ground floor, which used to house the factory foreman and his family. Or maybe one of the factory managers. That apartment is on the other side of the building, as far away from the factory as it could be. It was still mostly furnished, with old-fashioned, winged armchairs, and heavy wooden beds, chairs, tables, and wardrobes which were probably too much of a hassle to move after the building was abandoned. Much of that furniture was so old it would probably fetch a good price in the antique market, and I told her so. If she and the other women who lived here managed to sell some of it, they'd have enough to start a better life here. She didn't believe me.

A car rolls past the alley entrance behind me, sending my heart racing. I quicken my pace, but thankfully the hum of the engine fades off into the silence. I don't regret exposing this place and the prostitutes' way of life here. With prostitution being legal and regulated in Germany, it is only the most depraved men who came here to pick up these women who were working illegally and completely under the radar. The ones who liked to hit and bite and choke. To torture, in other words. And to kill? I'm sure there were more than a few of those too. Three of Selima's friends went missing in the eighteen months she lived and worked here and none of them were ever found again. It's good that the authorities cracked down on this place, and the one other similar spot my article exposed.

I should've just come to the building from the other side, along the wide main street, and gone straight to the apartment first. But I had a vague notion that it'd be easier to find a woman to talk to out in the street than by knocking on doors. The freezing wind is wailing through the empty alley by the time I reach the streetlamp in the middle of it. My heart is pounding so hard I'm breathless from it, and I still have to make it through half of this dark alley. And now I'm sure that the wailing is also masking the humming of a car driving slowly behind me.

There's nothing there when I turn, but there could be. A dark car with its lights off would be invisible here.

I'm just about to break into a sprint when the far opening of the alley explodes in light and sound. Sirens—police, ambulance, fire truck-are blaring, and the blue, yellow, red, and white flashing lights are illuminating the alley mouth like a New Year's fireworks display.

My heart's in my throat as I speed walk towards them, then break into a jog, my boots slushing in the puddles left by yesterday's snowfall and my feet kicking the trash that might have been here for a decade or more.

"Halt!" a young policeman yells as I burst from the alley onto the wide sidewalk on the other side. His face is awash in the blue and red flashing light. "You can't come this way."

"What's happening here?" I ask breathlessly.

"Stay back," he tells me, not answering my question and unrolls the yellow police tape he was using to cut off the alley from the sidewalk when I burst out of it.

It's not a fire, I would have felt and at least smelt that. But two fire trucks are blocking the main road leading past these two buildings, one on each side, their red flashing lights fighting the darkness, but not very successfully. Behind them on one side are the two police cars and an ambulance are joined by an additional ambulance and two more cars, all with their sirens blaring. And behind the other one, there's only a single police car. The silence that falls once all the sirens are turned off has a physical presence after all that noise.

A group of young men and women are huddled by one of the ambulances, wrapped in blankets while the paramedics work on them. The whole thing is overseen by three uniformed policemen. The flashing lights are reflecting off the many piercings in their ears, and on their faces. Smoke poisoning?

I take a step towards the yellow police tape that now stretches across the alley mouth and the edge of the apartment building where the policeman who stopped me is holding the roll, looking confused. He probably can't figure out where to attach the rest of it.

The silence is broken by the piercing sound of another siren coming from my right. It's not as loud as the others were, but promises more purpose as an unmarked detective car arrives, a tube light across the top of its windshield flashing blue. The car is followed by a black jeep with no siren and no flashing lights.

The wiry, thin and dark-haired Detective Schmitt gets out of the car with the flashing light. Mark steps out of the jeep. The detective doesn't look back at him as he makes his way towards the apartment building's main entrance which is standing wide open, only unbroken darkness on the other side, his hunched shoulders making him look even shorter, but his glassy dark eyes are blazing and full of purpose as he stares at his destination. Mark has to lengthen his stride to keep up.

Every part of me is screaming to call out to him. He's the only one who can bring me peace and calm in this cacophony of fear, noise, light, and movement, but I know he'll send me away. And I have to know if Selima is inside that building.

It's all pretty much in chaos with all the cars and people milling around, unsure what to do. I slip past the back of the young policeman who is still trying to figure out what to do with the rest of his yellow tape. I keep to the shadow of the tall building, my movement along the white-washed wall unremarked despite the flashing lights all around. Or maybe because of them. They do have a very disorienting effect.

The single uniformed police officer by the front door to the building is sent to do something by Schmitt who then slips inside followed closely by Mark. No one notices me follow them a few steps behind.

The only light in the huge, windowless entry hall is coming from the service cars outside, creating pools of light on the floor that are moving like actual water. They don't reach the far wall, which is shrouded in pitch-black darkness.

Mark and Schmitt are already out of sight when I enter, but I quickly spot a yellow beam of a flashlight Schmitt is carrying as he hurries down the corridor to the left of the entry hall. The corridor that leads to the foreman's apartment—Selima's apartment.

I hurry after them and almost run into Mark's back as I reach the wide-open doors of Selima's former apartment. They've stopped dead before entering, Schmitt's flashlight illuminating something I can't see because their backs are blocking my view.

"It's his work," Schmitt says curtly. "We wait for forensics."

I step sideways to peer through the gap between them. The beam of the flashlight is focused on a woman's face. She's kneeling on the floor by the fireplace in the large living room just beyond the small entry hall the front door opens into. Her face and what I can see of her white shirt is covered by dirt and dark grey ask. Her eyes are open, staring lifelessly at something on the floor.

It's not Selima.

I gasp as I realize that, my heart once again thumping in my throat, this time more in a mixture of relief and pure terror. Not a conformable mix of feelings.

Both the men turn to me, Schmitt's flashlight now blinding me.

"Who are you? What are you doing here?" he barks, just as Mark asks, "Eva? How did you get here?"

"I...I...came looking for Selima, you know the woman I interviewed for my article. The one who lived here," I stammer. "After reports started coming in that a body was found I was afraid it might be her so I came to see if she was—"

"Is this her?" Schmitt interrupts. "Is this the woman you know?"

He sounds on edge like the only thing holding him together is nerves of steel and cold, hard determination.

"No, it's not her," I mutter.

Mark moves to stand between Schmitt's flashlight and me. His face is all in darkness so I can't see his expression or his eyes, but I feel his caring, calm look anyway.

"Come on, you can't be here," he says as he puts his hands on my shoulders to turn me away from the door. I let him.

"I'll take you home," he says and wraps his strong arm around my shoulders and leads me out of the building. The floor feels like I'm walking on the surface of a very wavy lake.

Relief is still crashing against the absolute terror of just having witnessed one of The Fairytale Killer's creations first hand, from barely five meters away. Mark's strong body and protective arm are making it possible for me to walk out on my own. But only just.

It took me more than forty minutes to get to that alleyway by bus earlier, but Mark reaches my apartment building in fifteen. He rolls right onto the sidewalk, fast enough to make me bounce in my seat as we go over the curb. He hasn't spoken a word, his dark eyes reflecting the traffic and streetlights as he drove, looking straight ahead. Each time he glances at me, which was often, his eyes were kind like I know them, but laced with an edge of panic that I'm not used to seeing in them. A type of crazed terror, not unlike the one I'm still feeling.

He brakes hard, the jeep coming to an abrupt stop between my building's front door and the bus stop that's just to the left of it. He's around the car, holding my door open before I've even managed to reach for the handle to let myself out.

His arm around my shoulders is once again guiding me, this time up to my apartment. He's setting such a fast pace, I'm breathing hard once I'm finally unlocking my front door.

He passes me and heads for the kitchen. He has the bottle of Rakia and a single shot glass waiting as I follow him.

"Have a drink," he says. "You'll feel better afterward."

"I'm fine," I tell him, my faint voice and shaking hands painting that as a lie. But my legs are steady as I move to stand beside the kitchen table.

"What were you doing out there in the middle of the night?" he asks, his hands on my waist, their weight very welcome there, anchoring me in the here and now.

"I was just settling down for the night when all hell broke loose. My phones started buzzing non-stop, I was getting about five emails and notifications a minute, my editors were calling, friends and contacts were sending me pictures. Snow White was found this morning, and then what's her name, the Indian Princess by the river at dusk, and Snow White this morning," I look at him questioningly as I say it and he nods. "And I thought one of the girls looked familiar... she looked like Selima—"

"But it's not the Cinderella," he interrupts brusquely. "Which one then? Snow White?"

"No. It was...it was Sleeping Beauty," I say.

Mark's eyes narrow in confusion. "The one from before? In the tower? But we know who that one is and it's not your Bosnian prostitute friend. And we haven't found another Sleeping Beauty. How do you know about her?"

I'm getting lightheaded again. The cold and shock followed by the warmth and this uncharacteristic brusqueness and thinly veiled panic in the voice of the man I thought I could always count on being calm, steady, and collected are making me question just about everything about this night. But not the reason I went to that alley. I step out of the circle of his arms and pull my phone from my pocket.

I don't have to search for the photo that propelled me out the door, it's the last one I looked at.

"This one," I say turning the phone and thrusting it towards his face. "Sleeping Beauty at her spinning wheel. I think that's Selima."

He glances at the photo then looks me dead in the eyes. "How did you get this photo?" he asks.

The panic and concern in his eyes have been replaced by that soft calmness I like so much.

I shrug. "I don't know. It was sent to me via email, by one of my sources, I guess."

"Check who sent it," he says. The energy he's giving off reminds me of a guard dog's right before it pounces on an intruder and his eyes are all determination, no errant emotion left in them. Determination and anticipation.

"Why?" I ask. Over the years I've befriended a couple of police officers and a forensic criminalist. Sometimes they send me leads. I bet the photo was sent by one of them. "You know I can't reveal my sources, Mark. I can give you the photo, but why do you need to know who it's from?"

"Because we haven't found that crime scene yet," he says quietly, sucking all the air from the room.

I stumble back and sit in one of my kitchen table

chairs clumsily. Mark is pale, his eyes very dark as he looks down at me.

"Let me just see who sent it," I say, checking my phone for the email that had the photo attached.

"It was sent by MyPrincess@freemail.com," I say, looking up at him. "It's from one of those one-time email address providers. Untraceable."

"Forward it to me, I'll have my people try," Mark says brusquely.

The full implications of what just happened are raining down on me like pebbles hitting a calm lake until it's roiling by the time I'm done doing as he asked and forwarding the email.

"He sent me that picture, didn't he?" I say. "The Fairytale Killer."

Mark looks up from his phone, which buzzed with my email. His gaze is serious and searching, but calm caring is at the edges of all that.

"Not necessarily," he says. "It could be from one of your sources."

It sounds more like he hopes it is, not that he thinks it is.

"I don't want you to leave the apartment tonight," he says. "Lock yourself in and try to get some sleep."

A part of me wants to snap at him that I'm my own woman and can do whatever whenever I want. But that's a voice from before I started getting emails from a serial killer.

"All right, fine," I say. "But I have an article to write

for the Guardian. Can you at least tell me how many bodies you found?"

"Three, including Cinderella," he says. "But don't give this madman notoriety. It's what he wants."

He's told me this before and he got very mad when the press gave this murderer a nickname, saying monsters like this are in it for the fame and the more of it they get, the more daring they become. But how can a guy who kills young women and poses them to be perfect replicas of cartoon princesses fail to get a nickname? Still, I'll be glad when they find out this psycho's actual name.

"I'll stick to the facts," I say.

He shrugs. "That ship's sailed anyway. I have to go now. I'll call when I can."

I nod and walk him to the door, where he kisses me then hugs me so tightly it takes my air. But in a good way. In as much as anything can be good right now.

9

MARK

The night is turning to dawn, steel grey because of the thick clouds covering the city like the remnant of someone's nightmare and not the welcome coming of day. The German police department had received their own envelope of photos, similar, but not the same as the ones we got. Theirs was sent by post and addressed to the chief's secretary of all people. While we got a strand of hair with it, they found a single fingerprint in the corner of Sleeping Beauty's photo. They're running it now. I haven't gotten around to viewing the photos they got yet, to see if theirs matches the one Eva was sent. There's been too much else to do.

We've found three of the four crime scenes in the photos. But not Sleeping Beauty.

The frenzy of activity, of running from one crime scene to another, waiting for forensics to release each of them, waiting to see, not wanting to see, left no time to really wrap my mind around the scope of this thing.

Schmitt finally suggested we get some breakfast and coffee, so I've been trying to finish my plate of scrambled eggs, bacon, and toast. Everything tastes like cardboard, and the bacon is so hard, it's impossible to chew. I give up the struggle after having to swallow yet another piece of it whole and lean back in my chair, making it creak ominously, the cup of almost cold bitter black coffee in my hand. Drinking it has cleared my mind by virtue of being nauseatingly disgusting and not its caffeine content.

Across from me, Schmitt is finishing his own plate of bacon and eggs with robotic precision. His face is wearing its permanent scowl, and there's no way to tell if it's the poor quality of the food or the trail of gruesome death we're still just trying to follow that's causing it.

His phone buzzes with a text and he scowls at that too as he reads it while chewing methodically.

"They're ready to let us see Cinderella's crime scene," he tells me.

Around two AM I finally got clearance from Thompson to send our forensic people to the scenes to help with the workload, but it hasn't exactly sped up the processing of the crime scenes, since all it actually achieved is doubling the workload. Maybe that's for the best. With the lack of tangible, usable forensic evidence from the first two scenes, maybe we should double-up on collection from last night's three, the fourth pending. Maybe. But I doubt it. Leg work will solve this one, not fibers.

"I'm ready when you are," I tell him and finish the last sip of my coffee. I'm still recovering from its cold bitter sourness when my own phone rings.

The number's withheld, meaning it's not Eva, and that's about all I think before answering.

"This is Otto Blackman," a clear deep voice says on the other end of the line. "I've been going over the case files all night. Have you found the last body yet? Sleeping Beauty?"

Blackman arrived at the base at around ten PM last night and wished to arrange a meeting with me right away to go over the case. But we had just gotten the clearance to examine Pocahontas and reports were coming in that a group of squatters made a gruesome discovery in an abandoned apartment building. The last thing I wanted to do was go back to CID and have a quiet conversation. To be completely honest, with myself at least, ever since Thompson told me they were bringing in the legendary Otto Blackman to investigate this case, I've been plagued with a growing fear I'd be taken off it. Or at least pushed so far to the sidelines as to have no say in anything. Irrational, maybe. But I need to find this psycho. And I need free rein to do it.

"Good morning," I say, pausing to let all that fade in my mind.

"Good morning," he says curtly, his voice oozing displeasure at being reminded he forgot that simple courtesy when he called me. He probably considers it impertinence on my part, and his tone somehow clearly conveys that without being biting.

"So?" he adds, again leaving no doubt that he's not pleased with me.

Whatever.

"No, we haven't found her yet," I tell him.

"Did you check the German History Museum and the smaller one on Neue Christstrasse? The one that shows just the history of living in these lands?"

"Yes, we did," I say. The spinning wheel in Sleeping Beauty's photo looks authentic. This has been confirmed by both the CID lab as well as the German police.

We checked all the museums that could conceivably house an artifact like that, but it was a desperate act from the start. Ever since the first Cinderella was found on the outside steps of the Old National Gallery, the security in all museums in the city has been tightened so much that a mouse couldn't get in without someone knowing. I explain that to Blackman, using less colorful and more respectful language of course.

Quite possibly this madman purchased his own ancient spinning wheel from some antique shop just for the photo. Though his recreation of the cartoon and storybook scenes ends with the position and dressing of the body, since all the actual sites he incorporates into his sick visions are pre-existing places. As soon as I have at least the preliminary reports from yesterday's crime scenes, I'm going to sit down and go over everything again. There's got to be a thread running through all of this. Something I've been glimpsing since the start but can't quite wrap my mind around.

"Check the museum called Anna's Farm," Blackman says. "It's an old farm that's been converted into a museum showing the daily life of a German farming family. It's about ten kilometers out of the city on the road that leads to Snow White's cabin. From their website, it seems they have a whole room showcasing the old weaving process."

That's exactly the type of thing I should've thought of. But there had been too much input yesterday. Too much to think about.

"I'll send you the address," he says.

"Yes, please do," I say. "And I'll return to the office after we check this place. We can have a proper conversation then."

He murmurs something I can't quite make out but puts me in mind of a master who finally put his insubordinate underling in his place. Legendary inspector or not, I have a hunch I'm not going to like this Blackman. But he seems to still be as sharp as his reputation suggests, and whether I like him or not is irrelevant.

I tell Schmitt what Blackman told me and he's ready to leave within three minutes. A police cruiser joins us on the regional road that leads to this farm museum. Even the Berlin well-equipped and well-manned police force have been stretched thin by the crime scenes we found last night, and the single car is all that can be spared for the time being. Schmitt has already been trying to have reinforcements sent from nearby cities, and I have no doubt he'll get them. The German's are nothing if not efficient. Unfortunately, the man we're hunting is too.

The thick grey clouds are hanging even lower over the vast open countryside. We reach the farm museum just before seven AM. It's an old farmstead, meticulously renovated, the white-washed walls shining despite the lack of light. The museum consists of only three buildings—the main house, the barn, and the workshop. The house is a typical, stout, dark wood-paneled farmhouse that was once prevalent in this area—white walls, a brown thatched roof, and small windows with wooden shutters that have designs cut into them—hearts for the house, four-leaf clovers for the workshop. The barn has no windows. The complex is enclosed by a neat, new picket fence made of dark brown wooden poles. The fields all around it are covered by a thick, undisturbed blanket of fresh snow, but the road leading up to it and all the walkways between the three buildings were cleared of snow so meticulously that gravel and even tufts of grass are showing through in places.

Schmitt, the uniformed policewoman, and I are the only ones here. Schmitt tells the policewoman to keep trying to get in contact with the overseer of this place again, like we've been fruitlessly trying to do on the ride here with no success, then strides towards the gate in the fence. As I follow him, I feel like I could touch the thick clouds if I just stood on my toes, that's how low they are. They're carrying snow in their thick bellies and I've been hoping they'll hold on to it at least long enough for us to gather all the evidence from the exterior crime scenes before bursting. But after the vicious north winds of the past couple of days, the temperature is almost mild today, which is a sure indication that it's going to start snowing very soon.

Schmitt unlatches the gate and pushes it open. An objection that we should wait for the owner's permission before we go inside is on the tip of my tongue, but I swallow it. This is his show, and he knows the laws and which ones of them he can bend better than I do.

"The weaving room first?" he asks, looking at me over his shoulder, while already striding towards it.

The workshop is across the yard from the main house and to our right. A low rectangular building with slightly larger windows than the main house, though I suspect that most of the light the workers had to work in there came through the large door that dominates the narrower wall facing us. That door is bolted firmly shut and locked with a large dark grey padlock unless my eyes are very much deceiving me. Good. I'm sure we'll see well enough through the cutouts in the shutters on the windows and the padlock will prevent breaking any kind of unlawful entry and search problem.

Something's off about the main house though, I

vaguely notice from the corner of my eye as we pass it on the way to the workshop.

I stop and turn to look closer.

"Wait!" I say to Schmitt as I stare at the wide-open front door of the house. A light dusting of snow, which must have been blown in last night, is covering the dark entry hall.

Schmitt follows my gaze and gasps, then clears his throat to hide his shock. He's the kind of guy who tries very hard to always look composed, always hide his shock no matter how warranted it is. Only his red-rimmed, wild eyes betray it now.

"Let's check the house first," he says and makes his way across the yard to it.

We don't have to speak to agree that we're not going in via the front door, as that could compromise the little evidence this killer leaves behind. If he was here. Somehow, the nearer we get to the first row of windows there's no doubt in my mind that he was.

We peer through the heart-shaped shutters on the windows one by one, our eyes met with gloom and doom so deep I can barely make out the furniture. The large room to the left of the entry is the salon with a fireplace, a set of cloth sofas with a flowery design, and a hodgepodge of end tables, coffee tables, and lamps. The room next to it, the first on the narrow side of the house is a study, furnished with floor to ceiling bookcases covering most of the walls, and a large dark wood writing desk. Dark, but benefitting from the easter light.

A yellow flickering light is coming through the next window. An unshuttered window.

The first things my eyes meet are the dead blue ones of the girl we've been searching for all night. She's been positioned behind a spinning wheel, and she's staring wistfully out the window. Directly into my eyes. The madman posed her in different ways to take all those different photos. The realization hits me with a wave of nausea that threatens to bring the hard bacon and runny eggs I had for breakfast right back up.

Several fat white candles are standing on the table and windowsill next to her, some still burning, some just puddles of wax.

The room itself is cheery and pleasant, with a thick homespun rug covering the floor and a fireplace large enough to warm the whole small space on one wall. There's a comfortable looking winged armchair made of the same flowery cloth as the sofas in the salon in front of the fireplace and a matching one by the window where one could sit and read under natural light. The headrests of both are covered by white, lacy doilies which must have taken many an evening or morning to make. The spinning wheel the girl is sitting behind is smaller, a household sized one, which the lady of the house might have used to make what cloth her family needed while her husband worked on accounts in his study next door.

I never met Eva's prostitute friend Selima, but I saw her once from across a crowded coffee shop. She was leaving a meeting with Eva and I was just arriving to spend the rest of the night with her. I'm certain this is her. And of all the things I could and perhaps should be thinking right now, I'm most worried about how I'm going to break the news to Eva. She forged a very tight bond with the woman while she was interviewing her for the article, and even though they later fell out quite badly, Eva still hopes for a reconciliation. Hoped.

10

EVA

After Mark left my hands didn't stop shaking until after I had two shots of the Rakia he brought me from Kosovo. By the time I downed the second one I was ready to begin writing, and once I started gathering up all the information sent to me in various ways and by various sources, sentences and passages started unfolding in my mind. After I started typing, the work was all there was. No more worry, no more fear, just a cool, calm, and collected reporting of facts interwoven with my own observations, so much easier to see, understand and accept when they're words on a page and not suffocating fears in my throat.

I made Christina's deadline for The Guardian with half an hour to spare, then plunged right into two more articles for other venues. Sometime between the third and the fourth story I was working on, I rested my head on the table, promising I'll just close my eyes a few minutes to clear my head. But I fell into a deep sleep instead.

My phone ringing startles me awake, my flailing hand as I try to reach for it without opening my eyes fully connects with the shot glass, sending it flying into the wall where it crashes into a million pieces.

"Damn," I mutter just as I pick up the phone.

"Eva? Are you all right?" Mark sounds concerned. But vaguely so. Mainly he just sounds tired.

"Yes, I'm fine. Sorry about that, I broke a glass and it shattered. It'll take me at least an hour to clean it up," I hasten to explain.

"Sorry to hear that," he says flatly. "Did you get any sleep?"

"Some," I say, rolling my head to get rid of the crick in my neck from sleeping bent over the table. But motions only worsens the pain. "You?"

"No. Listen, I have to tell you something. Are you sitting down?" he asks.

"Yes," I say, letting my annoyance at his flat tone creep into my voice—or is it my fear and anxiety?

"We found Sleeping Beauty," he says. "And I'm 99 percent sure it is your friend Selima. I'm sorry."

I gasp into the silence, my heart racing so hard my chest hurts.

"I knew I recognized her," I mutter. "But I hoped I was wrong."

"Me too," Mark says, and for the first time since he called he sounds like the man I know and love, the man

I'm starting to seriously believe I could spend the rest of my life with. Caring and warm and calm enough to shelter me through any storm. Solid like the four walls of a happy home.

"You can't reveal that information yet, and I need to talk to you. You'll have to tell me everything you know about her. Where she lived, who her clients were, who she fought with, anything you can think of, I'll need to know it all."

"Yes, of course," I say, smarting at the pointed, almost harsh way he told me not to print anything about Sleeping Beauty—Selima—yet, but not enough to make an issue of it. I get it. He's not doing it because he doesn't trust me. He's just trying to do his job as best he can. "Are you coming here now?"

"Not yet, I have to go to the office first," he says, the brusque, businesslike tone back in his voice. "But I'll be there as soon as I can."

"OK, I'll be waiting," I tell him.

I do understand he has a job to do. A very important job. But as the line goes dead, I don't know how I'll face the silence as I process this news. Until this moment, The Fairytale killer was a faceless menace. Although he's by far the scariest psychopath whose criminal acts I've followed, there has been a safe distance between him and me. On some level, the murders were just another thing that was happening. Not so anymore. Now he's hit close to home. Now it's personal. Psycho bastard!

11

MARK

Otto Blackman was and remains the most efficient and effective investigator the US Military CID has ever employed. In his long career, he successfully solved more cases than any other two investigators combined, even things that were deemed unsolvable. His methods are studied, his cases are the basis for training, and no one knows exactly why he didn't at least stay on as an instructor after he left CID. Rumor has it that he was simply too burnt out and that he couldn't look at another crime scene without going into a nervous fit. But those are more whispers than anything else. And according to Thompson, they're completely off the mark.

I would tend to agree with that assessment, as he seems completely sound of mind and body as he looks up from the magical table in the forensics lab when I enter it. He was over forty when he retired—forty-seven if I remember correctly—which was almost twenty years ago. That would put him in his sixties, but if I didn't know that I'd say he was fifty-five at most. He's tall, but with a slim build that makes him unimposing, and his hair, though almost white grey, is thick and bushy. He has it combed back from his chiseled face in two lazy waves. His light blue eyes are alert and bright as he stands and offers me his hand in greeting.

"Inspector Novak, I presume," he says. "It's good to finally meet you."

"Likewise," I mutter, painfully aware of my disheveled appearance even though I haven't actually looked in the mirror yet. But I know my coat is wrinkled from getting in and out of the car all night, my face is covered with yesterday's five o'clock shadow combined with this morning's, and my hair is without a doubt a mess from running my hands through it over and over last night. It's a nervous tic of mine, doing that.

He nods and walks back to the table. I follow.

"I've been going over your case files all night," he says. "As I already told you on the phone. It's not much."

He has a rich clear voice, more treble than bass. He sounds like a radio announcer, and it doesn't quite fit with his physical appearance. I'd expect something wheezier or more high pitched from looking at him.

He has all the photos, reports, and lab results laid out in neat rows on the table. All of it together doesn't take up even half of the long workspace. The photos sent to Thompson occupy a row to themselves, off to the side of the rest. A paper map of the city and surrounding area is unfolded on the other side of the table, augmented with separate maps of the countryside. Clearly, Marisa hasn't been around to call up the maps he needs to the surface of the table digitally. A red circle marks the spot where Snow White was found this morning.

He's holding a blue marker, looking at me from beneath his arched brows. "You found the fourth body where I suggested? At Anna's Farm Museum?"

"Yes," I say. "It was right where you assumed it could be."

He walks to the map, removes a piece of clear tape from the farmhouse, and circles it with the pen. He then proceeds to remove several other pieces of clear tape from the maps, which were marking locations around the city.

"I'm glad my best guess as to her location proved the correct one," he says, crumpling the pieces of tape and putting them in his pocket. "But I had several other suggestions ready to go."

"It saved us hours, maybe days of work," I tell him flatly.

He's marked the other locations on the map as well —black for Cinderella, green for Snow White, and brown for Pocahontas. There are also several sheets of looseleaf paper covered with what can only be his slanted, spidery handwriting laid out with all the reports. Clearly, he's more of a looking at the pictures type of investigator. Personally, I think pictures can only tell you so much, at least they only tell me so much. I need to be out there, looking at the victims, looking at the crime scenes, looking potential suspects in the eyes. Bits of cloth, fibers, blood, and such never form a comprehensive enough picture in my mind. I have to live and breathe the case. That approach to things has been the source of many bouts of burnout for me and several people have suggested I should take a step back, keep myself removed, but I'm useless that way. And there's no way I'm trying that tactic with this killer.

"I would like to make it clear that I in no way wish to take over this case from you and relegate you to the sidelines," he says, his bright eyes so focused on me, I can't help but meet his gaze. "I understand all about getting possessive of cases, especially cases like this. This is still your case, Inspector Novak."

He has been reading the files. And in them all about the last few weeks of my hunt, where I well and truly lost my compass while grasping at all those straws.

I nod, thinking it'd be inappropriate to thank him, and pull out a chair beside his. With his attention to every single written and documented detail, and my willingness to go without sleep to investigate them, we could very well make a good team.

"So, what's your profile of this guy?" I ask, glancing at one of the sheets of paper covered with his spidery handwriting where he worked on that. I made a profile

—white, 30-50 years old, closer to fifty, highly functioning psychopath, mommy issues, misogynist, possibly with no priors, possibly a narcissist, though I'd expect one of those to start contacting the press and the police with attention-grabbing letters or phone calls by now. Though all the attention he's already been getting in the press worldwide could be enough for him.

I deliberately keep profiles vague, since constructing them is far from an exact science, they're most accurate in hindsight once the perpetrator has been caught and analyzed and they can lead you in a completely wrong direction. They're a breeding ground for making too many assumptions too soon, in other words.

He looks at the page with his notes and pulls it toward him. "From the nature of the crime and the actual crime scenes, I'd say we're looking for an older man, late forties, early fifties, most likely white, cold and calculated, methodical, yet somehow also possessing a very active imagination. Maybe married with grown children, possibly a widower. Something set him off, I would guess. I'd be very surprised if he's had any run-in with the police prior to this."

"Not that he's had a run-in with the police now," I interject wryly.

To look at him, Blackman is more off-putting than not, giving the illusion of the perpetually displaced professor, but his voice corrects that picture. It's rich and thick and has a very pleasant melody.

"You've interviewed a good number of people," he says.

"At least a hundred." I've not only interviewed but also re-interviewed most of them. "We questioned everyone from museum security guards to university professors, but all either had alibis, were out of the city or otherwise didn't turn out likely suspects. The one I liked best was Professor Weber, a classic literature professor at the Berlin University of the Arts who has a very deep obsession with fairytales. But my second interview with him was in his office at the university, and the mess in there pretty much convinced me he's not our man. His office was so cluttered with books and papers, and boxes of books and papers that his desk and bookshelves were barely visible. No way a disorganized man like that could craft those crime scenes. Plus, his actual fascination is more with obscure European fairytales, not the ones everyone knows, and especially not the Americanized versions of them."

Blackman nodded throughout my explanation, and he continues after I stopped talking.

"There's nothing disorganized about this killer, that's for sure," he finally says. "Except his choice of locations where he leaves the bodies. They're all over the map and with seemingly no other forethought than availability and vague connection to the scenes he's trying to evoke."

"Vague?" I ask, leaning back in my stool to get a better look at him. "Sleeping Beauty in the tower,

Cinderella cleaning a fireplace, Snow White in a forest…I wouldn't call those vague."

"Sleeping Beauty in a farmhouse?" he counters. "Cinderella on the steps of a museum that merely resembles a palace? Those are approximations, not up to par with his usual meticulousness."

"He doesn't have that many choices in Berlin now does he? Hardly any kind of medieval or Renaissance building is left after the whole city was razed by the Allies."

"Which begs the question, why Berlin? Why choose this city if it takes away from his creations in such an obvious way?" he says.

"Such an annoying way, more like," I say. "It's got to be because this base is here. It's the biggest US military presence in Europe and he clearly has a bone to pick with us. I had my suspicions about that from the start, that this was directly aimed at us, the US Military that is, but I was never able to prove that connection before they took me off the case. Well, I think Major General Thompson receiving those photos now proves it."

"Or the man is just local and knows this city like the back of his hand," Blackman muses. "He's been planning this for a long time, that much is clear."

He reaches over the table and pulls one of the photos towards us—Snow White with a man's back in the foreground. "And it seems he could be younger, much younger. Early thirties I'd say from this photo, maybe even younger."

The man in the photo has a broad back and chiseled

biceps and something in the easy, natural way he's holding his pose as he kneels on the floor by the bed suggests a young man in his prime. But it's not a very good photo of him.

The door from the corridor opens and people start filing in, some carrying cameras, others large bags over their shoulders. More than twenty of them stream in, greeting us before resuming their trek to the offices in the back. All have nearly identical ashen faces of people who had gone too long without sleep and seen too much. Eager Ross is the last to enter, his normally perky step and bright face just as ashen as the others'.

"You will start processing the evidence right away?" I ask him, though it's actually more of a statement, an order, really.

He nods. "Of course, sir."

The anticipation of getting new evidence in a case usually fills me with hope and a new wind to get back to the investigation. Now that anticipation is a sour knot in the pit of my stomach. By the end of the day, tomorrow morning at the latest, I'll be facing a pile, no, a mountain of evidence to sift through. That's how much of it there was after the first two cases, and I'm expecting more now. None of it led anywhere then, and I'm not hopeful that this new mountain of it will either. There'll just be a lot more of it.

"I'll stay here and wait for the evidence to be processed," Blackman says. "You go home and get some sleep. You look like you need it."

I nod as I slip off the stool. I have no intention of

going home or sleeping anytime soon, but I'm more than happy to let him sift through the preliminary evidence.

"Call me if you or they find anything," I say, and he assures me he will.

I do need sleep, I realize as I leave the lab and the grey walls of the corridor are flickering before my eyes the whole way. But my phone's been buzzing in my pocket practically the whole time Blackman and I spent talking, and I mean to find out what every one of those buzzes was about before I even think of going to sleep. In the first forty-eight hours we have the best chance of finding a lead, and we've already wasted more than half of them driving from one crime scene to another. But I'm still convinced that if this monster makes any mistakes, they'll be revealed right after the bodies are found, not weeks or months after. The last time, I didn't get the chance to be on the scenes right after they were found, but it's different now, and I'm going to make every minute count.

12

MARK

I asked Schmitt to meet me at the entrance to the park that surrounds the river where Pocahontas was found. It's the first one of the crime scenes and therefore the one that's already been released. The fat grey clouds are even darker now and there's even less light than there was at dawn.

As I wait for him, marveling at the mild weather after the cold of the last two days and thankful they were able to process this scene before the snowfall we're likely getting soon, the last of the police cruisers leaves. I'm suddenly alone here, and the peace of this place, the natural serenity, and the shifting pressure in the sky, no doubt are making me feel lightheaded.

It's not a bad place to die. Peaceful. Serene. Away from the noise and dirt of the city. But Pocahontas didn't die here. It's abundantly clear that this killer has a workshop somewhere, probably a big place, out of the way, abandoned in an abandoned part of the city. There's no lack of such places around here, and without a solid lead, we have no idea where to actually start searching for it. Even now, more young women could be dying there, being bled, photographed, defaced, prepared to be put on display. Treated like things, not people.

All night I've been detached, checking each scene methodically, storing the information, not letting the emotion of it in. Maybe that was a mistake. Either way, it's time to walk the path of this killer.

"Walk with me," I tell Schmitt as he pulls up beside me and opens his door. I don't wait for him to get out of his car before entering the park.

The path I'm walking is narrow and constructed of packed, crumbly gravel which is kept free of snow by virtue of the dense foliage and tall trees lining it. Most of them are leafless, but there are so many that their spindly, spiky branches still offer enough cover to protect the path from the snow.

Soon the path forks off into another path, and another after that, but I keep to the one I'm on. The one that will take me to the Havel river, which I can already smell. Water mixed with the decay of the countless leaves that found their way into it last fall, the freshness of the former not doing much to mask the latter. It's a natural smell, just like everything about this park is natural. Except for the princess.

"What are you hoping to see?" Schmitt asks as he

catches up. "The woman who found the body is down at the station, giving a detailed description of the only other person she saw here last night. A man. She even snapped a photo of his back. Don't you want to talk to her?"

"Later," I say and keep walking. There's very little evidence that people were working here all night and most of the morning, the tracks of the gurney which must have been used to transport the body to the hearse the most pronounced.

We round a bend, and the dark green waters of the river become visible behind the tall, yellowed grass lining it. Here too, the grass was shielded from the worst of the snowfall by tall, spindly trees growing everywhere with no seeming order. Along a narrow strip leading down to the bank, the grass has been trampled to provide access to the body, no doubt.

The only sound here is the slight hiss of the water. It's different in spring and summer, when there's no shortage of people walking and running here, but this is the dead of winter, quiet and peaceful. Anyone can do anything unobserved here in the winter.

I look around the way I wasn't able to when I first examined this scene, and everything was dark, except the princess and the scene around her which was illuminated by bright floodlight as the crime techs worked.

A narrowly steepled roof covered with white shingles is clearly visible amid the trees behind us, shining bright in the greyness of the leafless forest surrounding us.

"What's that place?" I ask. If I'm right, its tall windows have an unobstructed view of this riverbank.

I make my way toward it, cutting directly across the forest, without waiting for a reply.

"That's a teashop, but it's closed for the winter," Schmitt informs me. "There's no one there. No one was there since early November and there are no cameras. We checked."

But that's unmistakably a very human and very pale face watching me from one of the windows facing the river. Did The Fairytale Killer finally make a mistake and leave a witness? Is it possible?

The pale face in the window startled as soon as he, or she, saw me making for the teashop. The face disappeared to the left, the wide, large windows empty, reflecting just the trees and snow once again until I was sure I'd either seen a ghost or, more likely, no one at all.

"I work with the police!" I call out anyway once I'm within hailing distance of the house. "I just want to talk to you!"

No response. No movement. The tea house is a white wooden cabin with a narrow porch on the side facing the river. An area covered with slabs of concrete sprinkled with some sort of colorful scraps and shavings of a different type of material is probably where they put out the tables in the spring and summer, but right now it just looks like an unfinished porch that someone stopped constructing midway through.

Schmitt is breathing hard behind me, but even that is robotic and full of purpose—he needs more oxygen to reach his blood and he will do what must be done to achieve it, no more, no less. If this man was any more cool, calm, and collected, I'd be sure he was an android of some kind. It's why I investigated him as a suspect for the killings—because he fits the profile of a methodical, detail-oriented type.

I traverse the slabbed area and step on the low porch without using the steps. No lights are on inside, but the light spilling in through the large windows and double doors of the porch are enough to show me the whole space clearly. It's filled with round tables and chairs, all of which are made of wrought iron. The tables arranged in neat rows, the chairs stacked on the tabletops seats down, stretching from the porch door to the simple wooden counter that takes up the entire right-hand side of the space. Directly opposite the porch door, there's another one, leading into another part of the cabin. Through the window, I see yet another door further back open and close and someone streak through.

"Wait!" I yell and take off running around the cabin.

My quarry is a slight youth, with shoulder-length straight cut blond hair, wearing blue jeans and a large, checkered jacket that's at least two sizes too big for him. Or her. I can't tell. The person is also carrying a bulging black backpack on their back and a huge light grey duffel bag over his shoulders, as they try to run away from me, stumbling more than anything.

I have no trouble catching up with them. Only as I stop in front, blocking their path, do I realize it's a young man, looking about fourteen, though the pronounced whiskers on his cheeks put him at older. He looks at me with such angry defeat in his eyes, I'd say he was at least forty, if that's all I saw of him. He tried to run, but he failed. What he should've done is leave everything behind and made his escape. But I have a hunch that whatever is in those bags is all he has left in this world.

"I just want to talk," I tell him gently.

"About what?" he snaps in accented German. Polish? Russian? I can't tell.

"About what you saw down at the river," I say.

"I saw a bunch of cops working there all morning," he says. "You must know that. They're your friends, aren't they?"

"Colleagues, yes," I say, I have sympathy for this skinny kid with few choices, but his snarkiness is grating on my already very frayed nerves. That's definitely some type of Slavic accent, but the more he speaks the less pronounced it becomes.

"What about the night before, did you see anything then?"

"I only got there this morning, thought I could sleep in the teashop, get out of the cold. But I only went in after the cops left."

Schmitt caught up with us and is looking at the kid with his sharp black eyes as he works at regaining his wind.

"He's lying," he wheezes. "Either that, or someone else has made quite a nest in the back of that cabin."

The long sentence sends him back to square one in trying to regain control of his breathing.

I look at the kid sideways from beneath my eyebrows, saying nothing, waiting for him to start defending himself. They usually do, and they usually reveal a lot when they do.

His eyes aren't so angry anymore, or defeated, now they're mostly scared. I didn't think he was some hardened street kid when I first saw him, and this frightened look on his face confirms it.

"Fine, look," he says, looking down at his shoes. "I'm here as a student, but then my money ran out, and I lost my job and then I lost my apartment. I have a summer job at this teashop so I knew about the back room and I came to live here when I had nowhere else to go. It's been a cold winter."

I nod. "It has. And how long have you been squatting here?"

He looks at me sharply and I can just see his brain trying to come up with the best lie to tell me.

"I don't care about any of that," I tell him. "And I won't arrest you for trespassing or anything like that. I just need you to tell me the truth."

He glances at Schmitt and back to me, then swallows hard.

"I've only been here for one night," he says, not meeting my eyes. "I swear."

I turn to Schmitt. "I suggest you take him in for breaking and entering." Then I start walking away.

"Wait, no," the kid yelps amid rustling. "You said… you said you don't care about that…"

I stop and turn back to him. "I don't care about it as long as you tell me the truth. But you're lying."

It was just a hunch, but his wide-eyed, open mouth glassy stare tells me I was right on the money.

"Fine, all right," he says in a quiet voice. "I've been here since just after New Year's." He looks down at his scuffed boots again. "And I suppose you want to know about the dead woman by the river…" He pauses and looks at me questioningly. I nod. "…and who I think left her there."

13

EVA

I'm seriously regretting that I didn't take my bike. The weather's holding, growing hotter, not colder, and I doubt the snow will come today at all. Consequently, I'm also regretting wearing my long down jacket. My cheeks are hot, I'm starting to sweat and I'm not even halfway to my destination, which is a series of narrow streets and alleys at the end of this long, wide, and practically deserted avenue. Only a handful of cars have passed me since I started my trek, some slowing to ride beside me for a while. Probably some trick looking for a good time. I kept my eyes on the dark grey, pitted sidewalk beneath my feet and kept trudging on.

Berlin might have been built in the middle of total flatlands, but they still angled the streets to aid rainwater and snowmelt flow and these slight elevations

THE FAIRYTALE KILLER

are seriously making my thighs ache. I'll be achy all over tomorrow. I just hope it'll be worth it.

I've been searching the areas around where Selima lived and worked for hours. It's past two and it'll start getting dark soon. And dark is not a good time to be walking around these parts. Not that actual dusk will look much different from how this whole day has been with those dark, thick grey clouds hanging ominously low over the city all day.

And after four bodies in one day, I'm thinking even The Fairytale Killer needs a day off. Fear has been a constant presence all around me and especially in the knot in my stomach all day.

The area I'm making my way towards is my final destination and I'll splurge on a taxi to get back home. If I find Selima's friends here, it'll be money well spent. If not, I'll kick myself for being an idiot.

I'm not sure if the tall, communist-era buildings lining this main avenue are even occupied or not, though the few lighted windows and grimy signs here and there suggest that someone is still struggling to do business here. I pass a kebab shop, with a bored-looking man in a large white apron and white cloth cap, staring out the windows at me. The slab of meat is rotating on its spike behind him, and I wouldn't eat there if someone offered me a million euros. Well, maybe for a million. The man doesn't even see me, I don't think, he's just staring right through me as I pass his shop's windows and it sends an eerie, foreboding kind of feeling through me, doubling the sense of dread

I came here with and which no amount of sarcasm can lift.

I finally reach the warren of alleys I'm heading towards. The car—a blue Renault hatchback—which slowed to check me out on my trek here is parked next to a trash dumpster in a narrow lot between two dark brown brick buildings. I can just make out two people sitting in it. The trick and one of the girls. As always, sadness drenches me. How low they've fallen, reduced to having sex with strangers next to the trash. So many view them as being no better than trash, like with like, I'm sure most are thinking, but no one says it because everyone and everything is so politically correct nowadays.

Selima would say it. She always called it how she saw it and never tried to hide from the reality of her situation. It's one of the things I liked most about her.

The warren of alleys and narrow streets forms a tiny sort of square here, and light from a small coffee shop in one corner is spilling out onto it.

I can hear talking from the inside before I even reach the front door. But as soon as open it and a bell chimes over my head, all conversation stops dead, every head turned towards me. Well, the heads of the four young women sitting in the far corner, crammed around a small round table, wearing so little I shiver despite being so overdressed. It's not exactly cold in this place, but it isn't warm either.

An older, very fat man is behind the counter, his light eyes tiny inside the folds of his face. He wipes his hands on his apron, which is stretched taut over his oversized belly. That apron is dirty, stained brown, black, yellow, red, green, and other colors I don't even have names for.

"Are you lost or something?" he asks mockingly, leeringly.

"I'm looking for a woman named Selima," I say. No sense telling them she was found dead this morning. Even I'm not ready to fully accept that yet, and asking for her like this makes hope flare in my chest. Even though it's a lie.

"Selima is not here," a black-haired woman wearing much too much gold sparkly eye shadow says curtly and turns away from me. I know her vaguely. I also recognize two others around the table. Only one of them is a complete stranger.

I walk over to them and stop where they can all see me. "You must remember me. I'm Eva—"

"Yes, Eva the reporter," the black-haired one snaps. Her long hair is a tower atop her head, and she's wearing a tight, faux leather dress, fishnet stockings, and black stilettos. She could pass for a rock fan dressed up for a night of clubbing, or a model, with those long legs and pretty face. "Selima never wants to see you again. Now run along before something happens to you here."

The threat isn't an idle one, but it's meant more as a warning that this is the bad part of town and not that she, the three women with her and the fat man will harm me physically.

"Please, Ana," I say, finally remembering her name. She's Hungarian, and she did come here to be a model. "I need to see Selima, it's urgent."

I'm on the verge of telling them Selima's dead and I'm looking for information on who her killer might have been. These women spent so much time together, they knew of each other's every movement. It's how they kept each other safe working the streets with no protection from the state or even pimps. One of her friends saw her leave with the man who killed her. And when Mark comes to question me about her later, I mean to have more than just her description and the names of her friends to give him. It's why I'm here, even though I have a ton of articles to write. To help him catch this psycho.

"I am not talking to you. None of us are," Ana snaps, and shoots to her feet, looking down at me from her stiletto heel augmented height. I look back into her eyes, into the abyss of rage and aggression. "You and your stupid article is the reason only the nastiest Johns come looking for us here. And not even every day."

Maybe I was wrong. Maybe she would hurt me physically. Her blazing eyes sure are saying she'd like to.

But she's the first to break our eye contact. "Come on, girls," she says to the others. "There's work to do."

She jostles past me, knocking me into the chair behind my back.

I look after her, my mouth open to speak, but I can't very well yell out that Selima's dead and they might know who the killer is. The man behind the counter isn't the only other person in here. A greasy-haired, skinny guy in a flannel shirt and jeans so washed out they're nearly white slumped over a table by the door, and a couple of wiry, short men with greasy black hair talking quietly two tables down. Or they were talking, now they're staring at me too.

The door closes behind Ana and my chance is gone. I could follow, I could find her outside and tell her why I'm really here, but that wild rage in her eyes makes me seriously doubt it would be a good idea.

"I want to know where Selima is too," a thin voice says behind me in very poor German. I look to find the fourth girl, the one I don't know from before still standing by the table. "Meet me at the kebab place. We'll talk then. I have to follow Ana now."

She leaves, swaying precariously in her bright red stiletto pumps, which look to be at least two sizes too big for her. She's wearing a tight dress, made from a vinyl type material, that barely covers her butt, and a short fake fur jacket which comes down to her cinched waist.

I give her a head start, but as soon as the women are gone all the men in the place are glaring just at me, so I leave too. Ana and the rest of them are nowhere to be seen and I practically jog back out onto the avenue and to the kebab place to wait. For what I hope is the first step on the road to catching Selima's killer.

14

MARK

The air isn't moving, and there's a slight humming in the air, as though coming from the low-hanging clouds, the snow in them roiling and boiling, ready to get out. I feel that tingling on the back of my neck like we're being watched. And we might be. The spindly trees around us are so dense and growing so haphazardly anyone or anything could be hiding in the shadows they cast.

"Let's go back to the teashop. Talk inside where it's warm," I tell the kid and bend over to pick up his duffel back. He snatches it away before I can though, the effort sending him stumbling backward and almost falling on his ass.

I shrug and let him precede me towards the teashop. Laden as he is with his body weight in belongings there's less of a chance he'll try to run again.

The back of the teashop is a larger space than I would've expected, separated into two rooms leading from the narrow hallway. The door to one of them is firmly shut, but not to the other. Inside it, I can see a rumpled up sleeping bag, several empty bags of chips, plastic sandwich wrappers, and empty coffee cups. The remains of at least two dozen candles are also strewn all over the place. I lead the way in there.

There're no shutters on the windows here and behind the door, there's a sturdy but plain wooden desk, an old office chair, and several metal filing cabinets lining the wall behind it. He's also brought a couple of the wrought-iron chairs back here, and a pair of light blue jeans are hanging off one of them, while the black rag under another is probably one of his hoodies which he forgot in his haste to get away.

"Sit," I tell him, pointing at one of the chairs.

"So what's your name?" Schmitt asks him curtly.

The kid's eyes flitter to him then settle back on mine. "Jakob."

"Jakob what?" I ask, not unkindly. He's scared and I see no reason to make it worse. But my heart's pounding so hard I feel it hammering in my chest. This could be the break we've been waiting for, so I need this kid to start talking fast.

"Jakob Dabrowski," he adds, swallowing hard.

"So what did you see?" It's an effort to keep my voice friendly and light. But I know witnesses and even suspects respond better to calm friendliness, and I'll need this kid to tell me every tiny little detail he can remember.

Instead of speaking, he's just looking at me dumbly, his eyes wide, his mouth slightly open. I nod to encourage him.

"OK, so, yeah," he says, wiping his palms on his jeans. "I was only just falling asleep when I hear footsteps outside. It was after midnight and very dark. It was unusual. Hardly anyone comes here during the day in the winter and no one comes during the night. The man was huffing and grunting and talking. I was afraid they were coming to the teashop, that maybe it was a couple of gays looking for a place to…you know…" his pale cheeks turn a peach color as he flashes me a glance.

I nod. "So there were two men, not one?"

He shakes his head. "I crawled to the main room to hide behind the bar. The footsteps were coming from the back and I figured I had a better chance of escaping through the windows there. But no one came in. And the man just kept walking, didn't even stop at the teashop. So I went to the window to see where he was going. It was just one guy, carrying something on his shoulder, something heavy judging by the curses he was spewing and his hard breathing."

"Something like a body?" I ask.

He shrugs. "It was slung over his shoulder. But not hanging down his back. It looked like a camera on a tripod. But bigger than any I've ever seen."

"And he went down to the river?" I ask.

"Yes. After a while I lost sight of him in the darkness," he says. "But then, about thirty minutes later, a camera flash went off several times. That's how I figured he was probably carrying a camera. And then a light came on, a white light like they use on film sets. It lit up the river bank and the grass around it, almost to the path."

"Did you get a good look at the man then?" I ask, sounding eager despite not wanting to. My heart's thumping harder and harder.

He shakes his head, the shock stopping my racing heart dead. "I didn't see him at all in the light. And while he walked past here, it was so dark that all I could see was his shape. He was wearing dark clothes and a dark hat. But he was a big man, tall and broad across the shoulders. Not fat, but built, you know."

"How tall was he?" I ask. "My height."

Jakob eyes me appraisingly. "Yes. Maybe a little taller but not much."

I'm six foot two. In places like Italy or Spain, even Holland, and France, that kind of information might narrow down our suspect list. But Germans, especially in the north, are tall, and a lot of them are built, as the kid puts it. A built guy huffing and puffing carrying just a tripod and camera though? That makes no sense. Though maybe the kid's fear made him seem louder than he actually was. I bet a whisper carries in the nighttime silence here.

"Anything else you can tell me? Anything else that struck you?"

The kid nods. "Yes. The man was speaking English. And it wasn't a German speaking it. He sounded just like they do in the movies. Hollywood movies."

"What? He was talking to himself?" I ask. "Or was someone else with him?"

"I didn't see anyone else. Maybe he was speaking on the phone, but I didn't see a phone," he explains.

"And he was speaking American English?" I ask and the kid nods.

Schmitt is eyeing me pointedly, and I return his gaze. For all his pointed looks and robotic movements, his eyes and face are actually very expressive. Right now he's thinking, "I knew this monster is an American", and I hear that as clearly as if he spoke the words.

The thing is, I've been suspecting the same thing for months now. I just haven't told anyone yet.

15

EVA

I make my way out of the tangle of alleys onto the main avenue. Ana is further down it to my left, I recognize her by the tall tower of hair on her head which together with the rest of the black outfit makes her seem impossibly tall.

The woman who said she wanted to talk about Selima is by the kebab place, leaning on the wall and pretending not to notice me as I walk up.

"You got a car?" she asks once I'm standing next to her, without looking at me.

"No," I say. "Do you know where we can go to talk?"

"How about the city center?" she says, her eyes bright and hopeful.

"Great, let's find a taxi," I say, scanning the road for one. "We can have some early dinner while we talk."

I had the dried end of a baguette dunked in half a

cup of yogurt this morning after Mark left, and even that just so I could say I ate something. Truth is, I'm not really hungry now either, but I'm lightheaded and jittery, which means I should eat.

"There are no taxis here," she says and giggles. "At least not ones picking up passengers. You have to call one."

I have several taxi services saved in my phone and do as she suggests, calling the one that's usually the fastest and most reliable. She wanders away from me, telling me we shouldn't be seen talking by Ana while we wait for a cab. I have no idea how she plans to explain getting into the cab with me when it arrives, and almost ask her, but then a car pulls up next to Ana —a black Audi station wagon—and she gets in without even checking who's in it. Clearly a regular.

It's still a long fifteen-minute wait for the taxi to arrive after that, during which the kebab guy comes out, a leery look in his eyes and a fake wide smile on his lips as he not so suavely offers the girl some food, strongly suggesting he'll take payment in kind. He's flirting, I realize after watching the woman giggle and coyly lead him on. He's about her age, I think, which is very early twenties, if that. The more I watch them interact, the more I believe this isn't the first time they've done this. Maybe good things do happen on this street.

The cab arrives, and the girl says goodbye to the guy hurriedly, then climbs into the car before me.

"I'm Eva. What's your name?" I ask her after I give

the guy directions to a small restaurant near my apartment.

"Mirela," she says, and I don't think it's a made-up name.

"And where are you from?" I ask. I have a hunch, and when she tells me Velika Kladusa, the same place Selima was originally from, it's confirmed. I tell her that in my not stellar, but adequate Serbo-Croatian, asking if that's where she knew her from. It's not exactly the same as Bosnian, her native language, but it's close enough.

"Selima is my cousin," she tells me in her native language, visibly relieved I speak it too. Her German isn't very good. "You could say I followed her here then followed in her footsteps too. She never lied about what she was working as here, nor did she ever tell me it's an easy life. But it's easier than back home, you know?"

In her eyes there's a mix of hope, shame, and innocence so naïve, I have to steel myself not to look away from her questioning gaze. I get that look a lot when interviewing those on the edges of society, or beyond that edge, people in professions that most people scoff at, and look down on. She's trying to justify herself, explain to me that she has no choice but to be a prostitute, that she knows it's wrong, but it's her only option. I squeeze her hand, which is frail and very cold.

"I understand," I tell her. "And you don't have to explain yourself to me."

We've exited the run-down neighborhood she

works in and entered the lively, relaxed one where we're headed. The streets are full of people despite the winter gloom hanging over the city, and more than a few cafes lining the sidewalks have tables outside which are also full of people, chatting and laughing and just generally enjoying themselves. This is a hip, young, diverse neighborhood in Berlin, up and coming and still cheap to live in. I live just a few blocks from this area and often come to the cafes to work when my apartment starts feeling like the box of loneliness and isolation it is. Mirela is looking out the windows with wide, happily interested eyes, her lips slightly parted.

The cab pulls up to the curb and I pay then climb out, Mirela right behind me.

"I don't feel out of place here at all," she says, checking out the street. "That woman's skirt is even shorter than mine."

I look where she's pointing, and she's not wrong. The punk girl is wearing a short red and black plaid schoolgirl skirt, with ripped fishnets and army boots. I shiver just thinking about going out in fishnets in winter, but she seems not to notice the cold as she chats with her friends—a girl dressed similarly as her, and two guys in tight, ripped black jeans. At a table next to them, a man with long, greasy hair and wearing baggy, wrinkled jeans is having coffee with a young businesswoman in a tight skirt and blazer under a long, wool coat, the belt of which is almost touching the sidewalk. That's what I love about this neighborhood and this city in general. Everyone is welcome, no one is out of place. I guess it comes out of the bitter experience of being the aggressors in the worst war that the world has ever seen, coupled with living in a divided city for so long, the two sides as starkly different as day and night.

"I thought you'd feel most comfortable here. I know I do," I tell her. "The restaurant is this way."

Mario's is not an Italian restaurant as the name suggests, they cater to every taste. Lately, they've even started offering vegan and raw stuff, which I tried the last time I was trying to start living healthy, but it didn't stick. It's a small, homely place, with scuffed hardwood flooring and scratched tables and chairs that have seen a lot of use. The rough white walls inside have long since turned yellow from the heat wafting from the pizza oven, and all the cigarettes smoked in the small space before smoking indoors was outlawed. Pictures of celebrities ranging from Mike Tyson to Mickey Mouse line the walls.

I take her to a table in the back, in the shadow of the pizza oven, where we'll have some privacy, but also a great view of all the other people in here. She starts soaking it all in as soon as she sits down.

"They all seem so relaxed and happy," she says after the waitress brings us the menus. "I miss that. It's still like that in Sarajevo sometimes, but not in my village. There every one just complains and bitches all the time. I thought it'd be better here, but so far, I've only been to those run-down places in those rundown alleys where we, you know…" that look of shame again. It turns my stomach. "And everyone bitches there too, especially now that the police have started patrolling the area so much and arresting everyone there."

She doesn't add that they think it's because of my article, and I'm thankful for that. It's really not. It's because of The Fairytale Killer and the fact that his preferred victim is an illegal prostitute, but I won't mention that. It'll just scare her.

"I can help you get off the streets," I tell her.

She shrugs and gives me a sad little smile. "I'm happy enough."

The waitress comes back and she orders a vegetable soup, a large pizza, a chocolate milkshake. I get the yellow curry, which is the best I've ever tasted anywhere, even though this place offers such a hodge-podge of food that there's no way they could ever be masters of just one.

"When was the last time you saw Selima?" I ask, thinking I'll return to offering her help after she knows about the full scope of the danger the streets of Berlin currently pose.

She thinks about it for a while, nodding her side to side. "On the third of January. We had coffee at home and sat and talked for hours. Just like old times, before we both lived here."

"And then you went to work and never saw her again?" I ask.

"I went to work. It was a very windy and freezing kind of night and so cold even most of the Johns stayed home. I had a total of one client in four hours and then

I decided I'd rather be warm and hungry than cold and paid, so I went home. I expected Selima to already be there since I didn't see her on the street, but she wasn't."

"And home is the apartment building next to the factory?" I ask. The place where we found Cinderella. I wonder if she knows about that. She doesn't seem to.

She shakes her head. "No. That place was grand, but we had to move after the police raided it. We were in an abandoned three-story house near where you found me today. Me and the other girls still live there now."

"Where do you think Selima could've gone that night?" I ask. "Don't you girls keep an eye on each other?"

"Selima did things her own way, and she had secrets. Her hot soldier boyfriend being the chief one of them. I was the only one who knew about him."

"Tell me about him," I say, but her soup arrives just then, and she digs in with a relish I haven't seen since I watched the last young and very hungry child eat. She's not talking and I don't have the heart to force her to stop eating.

So, Selima had a boyfriend that she was keeping secret from everyone. Did she consider him a way out for her? Her one and only plan of getting out of the street life was to meet a guy and marry him. She was never interested in me helping her get a residency permit, which would allow her to get a real job. I figured I'd have time to convince her. Now that time's run out. The knot that forms in my throat is so hard I have trouble breathing, let alone swallowing. It's a good thing I wasn't served yet.

"What did you ask me?" Mirela asks, pushing the empty soup bowl away and wiping her mouth with the back of her hand before thinking to use the napkin by her side.

"The man Selima was seeing, tell me about him," I say ignoring the waitress who comes to take the empty soup bowl and hoping the rest of the food won't arrive right away.

"He was a big guy, very good looking, muscular, a good catch. Blond, blue-eyed, typical all-American jock, you know," she says and I nod. I don't really know, but I bet she does. There's no shortage of US military presence where she comes from, she must know all about jocks.

Her pizza and my curry and rice arrive, but I don't touch it.

"Was he a soldier? An American soldier?" I ask. That description sure makes it sound like that.

"Yes, and I was surprised when she told me," she says, pausing to take a bite of her pizza. It came pre-sliced, and she's holding it folded over double the way Mark eats his. Where I come from, we use a fork and knife to eat a pizza, but I like this method.

"Why?" I ask to nudge her along since I don't want her to stop talking again.

"You know, soldiers are always just looking for a good time, and you can't count on them for anything," she says.

"So I was surprised that Selima was so serious about him. But he was apparently from a rich family. Though that could've been a soldier lie. They're known for those too."

Mark is the only US soldier that I've ever gotten to know well, and he's the most truthful person I know. But then again, he is older.

"How old was this man?" I ask.

She shrugs, taking a large bite of pizza and chewing slowly.

"Younger than thirty, I'd say," she finally says. "But I don't know exactly."

"And do you know his name?"

"Russell. I remember that because it's such an old man's name and didn't fit him at all," she says while still chewing. "His last name started with a P, something weird like Parcibal or something like that."

I've never heard that last name.

"And how sure are you that he was the last person to see Selima alive?"

"You think she's dead?" Her eyes go very wide. If I could, I'd kick myself so hard I'd scream out. The names of the last four victims haven't been revealed yet. I only know it because Mark told me off the record.

I smile and shake my head. "Sorry, I got carried away there. I don't think she's dead…well…well…we don't know what happened to her now, do we? And my thoughts just always go to the worst possible scenario, I'm weird like that."

I smile in a way that I hope isn't transparent at all. Eventually, she offers me a tiny little smile too.

"I've been thinking that too," she says, letting the crust of the slice she was eating fall to the plate and not picking up another.

"It's hard not to, but she might just be having a good time with this guy, you know," I say so hopefully I almost believe it's a possibility myself.

She shrugs. "I don't know…"

"Come on, finish your pizza," I say, finally picking up my fork. "Then I'd like you to speak with my boyfriend. He's an investigator and has been helping me look for Selima. He'll want to know what you just told me."

My heart is thumping so hard I can't take a full breath, let alone take a bite of my food. Mark once told me that in every investigation they always focus on the victims last 24 hours and especially on the people they were with last. This usually holds the key to solving the crime. Could Mirela be the key that finally leads to catching The Fairytale Killer? I dare not hope it, but I do.

"OK, yes, that'd be good," she says and picks up another slice. Her eyes aren't innocent anymore, or happy. They're sharp as she gazes into mine, as though she's trying to read what I'm not telling her. I keep my face as neutral as I can while I eat my curry.

Mark hasn't called me all day, but I'll call him as soon as we're done eating. He needs to hear Mirela's story.

16

MARK

Jakob protested and fought when Schmitt told him we need to take him with us to the station, but he had no other choice and between us, we managed to drag him and his belongings to the parking lot at the entrance of the park. There was no other choice for him because he's the closest thing to a witness we'd found in this case, and we are therefore not letting him out of our sight. Schmitt and I barely had to glance at each other to agree on that.

The sky is a few shades darker than it was all day as I follow Schmitt's dark grey Volkswagen sedan. The thick, snow-laden clouds are still hanging low over the city, and the night is settling. It's been twenty-four hours since Pocahontas' body was found and the more I consider it, the more it seems to me that she could be the key to catching this madman. I had the first kernel of that idea as soon as I saw the photos in Thompson's office and finding our first eyewitness kind of confirmed it. She's the only one who doesn't fit with the others.

Pocahontas wasn't a princess in the true sense of the word, and she's not a fairytale princess either. She was the daughter of an Indian tribal chieftain, and if I remember correctly, she was an actual person who died very young and inspired many works of fiction, including the cartoon. Either The Fairytale Killer is branching away for fairytales as inspiration for his kills, or she's a message. I'll just treat her as such and hope I never have to find out if the former is actually the case. That's why I chose to revisit her crime scene first.

Some time between finding the fourth body early this morning and talking to Otto Blackman, I came to the conclusion that the best way to go about solving these murders is to focus on one and dig. I was going to suggest that to Schmitt at the park, but then we found the eyewitness. We already wasted a good part of these first twenty-four hours by visiting the different crime scenes, conferring with lab techs, and generally doing too much busywork.

Gatow, the area where we found the body is a good distance from the city center even when there's no real traffic, but this is the evening rush hour so it takes us almost two hours to arrive at the station even with taking all the back roads Schmitt knows.

Jakob has moved on to cursing us in his native

language by the time we reach the station and Schmitt wastes no time getting a couple of uniforms to take the kid inside the station.

I follow them inside, up the five concrete steps, which are awash in blue and white colors reflecting from the large sign over the door, proclaiming this building as a police station. It's the biggest one in the city, more a headquarters building than just a station, but that's not what the Germans are calling it. It's housed inside a tall, narrow but long, boxy building of the type that was architecturally so popular in the 1950s. It rises ten stories, with 30 offices per floor. The Homicide unit takes up the entire third floor. The entrance to the building is made up of three revolving doors and two large freight doors on either side. I follow Schmitt though the left most revolving door into the reception area, which is dominated by a long counter with five uniformed police officers manning it. To the left and right of it are three rows of wooden benches for those waiting to be seen. There's not that many today. A man with jet black hair and wearing a rumpled, but expensive dark blue suit with no tie and the front of his white shirt unbuttoned, is alone on the left side of the reception counter. A dark grey coat, also expensive-looking, is taking up the two seats next to him, thrown on there so haphazardly that a third of it is trailing on the floor. A woman in a long, military green parka is sitting on the other side of the waiting area, along with a group of six distraught, frightened-looking tourists talking in hurried Italian, and a dwarf off by himself. The police station proper can be accessed by two sets of black steel doors also on either side of the counter, which can only be opened with a code.

"Detective Schmitt," the uniformed woman sitting in the center spot behind the counter calls as we pass her on the way to the doors.

Schmitt's facial expression doesn't change, but something in his eyes tells me beyond doubt that he resents this interruption.

"What is it?" he asks the woman sharply.

"There's two people who want to see you right away," she says.

"Why? Who?" Schmitt asks. He's never one to waste words.

The police officer nods at the woman in the green coat. "That's the one who found the body in Gatow yesterday. She says she remembered something that can't wait."

Then she nods in the other direction. "And that man is convinced one of the victims you found last night is his daughter. His name is Vladimir Alexeyev."

I turn to look at the man more closely, recognizing the name. He's the head of the most prominent Russian mob family working in the city, the leader of a syndicate of Russian mobsters, actually. If he wasn't here alone and if his hair wasn't messed up like he's been running his fingers through it all afternoon, I'd probably recognize him.

Schmitt merely glances at him. "Send them both up after us."

Then he continues walking to the door.

"Are you Detective Schmitt?" the man bellows, his German accented but clear. "Are you the one investigating the murders?"

He gets up and strides towards us, and since there's no way to ignore him, Schmitt turns and faces him. "Yes, I am."

"I demand to know if one of the victims is my daughter," the man says. "I've been kept waiting for two hours and I won't wait a minute longer. Is this her?"

He pulls a photograph from his right pocket, showing us a picture of a fifteen, maybe the sixteen-year-old girl in a dark blue school uniform. She has bright dark brown, almost black eyes, and long, straight black hair, which is shorter than our Pocahontas'. But that's only because this picture is a few years old. It's the same girl, and it makes me very sad that she'll never smile this brightly again.

Schmitt glances at the photo and then me, and it seems that's all the answer to his question the man needs.

"No! Not my Nadia!" he bellows with such raw grief I feel it too. Painfully.

"Come with us. We'll talk upstairs," I tell him instinctively, despite the fact that I'm just an observer here and have no ability to make any such decision. But Schmitt confirms it and walks to the door, punching in the six-digit code to open it.

The elevator ride up to the third floor is the longest and most uncomfortable one I've ever taken. The man is looking at the photo, clutching it so hard his knuckles are white and I can literally feel his struggle not to start screaming.

"This way," Schmitt says once the elevator opens and then leads us to a small, informal interview room at the end of the hall. Inside it, there's a round table with a white plastic top and six blue chairs around it, and it smells of old polyester carpet, plastic, and stale coffee. Clearly, no one has opened the windows in here for quite some time.

"Mr. Alexeyev, please sit," Schmitt says, and the man does, looking grateful that he can. And defeated. His hands are still clutching the photo, but they're shaking now. "I can't confirm that we found your daughter's body last night," Schmitt continues in that monotone, almost robotic voice of his, but it's spot on right now.

"We did, however, find several bodies, I am sorry to say, some of which we have yet to identify. If you tell me why you suspect one of them might be your daughter, I can arrange for you to go and try to identify her," Schmitt continues, handling the situation perfectly, as far as I'm concerned. We won't get much out of Alexeyev if he's stricken with grief over his daughter's death, and he clearly knows something, else he wouldn't be here.

"Yes, good," Alexeyev says and visibly relaxes. He even lays the photo down on the table, smoothing out the wrinkles he caused as he clutched it.

"What made you think your daughter's body has been found?" Schmitt asks.

I take a seat to Alexeyev's left and Schmitt follows suit, taking a seat to the man's right.

"Nadia, my daughter, she's been acting out lately. She just turned eighteen last December, and she thought she was grown now and in charge of her own life. Even though she's still in school. We fought, she ran away, and I haven't seen her in almost two weeks. I had my men out looking for her, but they couldn't find her anywhere. Then I get a call from the station telling me that you did."

"Who called you?" Schmitt asks, a little too sharply perhaps.

"Someone I know," the man says evasively.

It stands to reason that a man as powerful as Alexeyev would have informants in the police. I can see that Schmitt is about to go down that line of questioning with him, and I forestall him by asking, "Where was your daughter last seen?"

Alexeyev fixes me. "In one of those filthy squats in Friedrichshain a week ago. Two of my men found her there, and they almost managed to catch her and bring her back, but she was with a guy. Military, by the sound of it. He took out both my guys and ran away with my daughter."

Schmitt and I exchange a look.

"A tall, muscular guy?" I ask. "American?"

Alexeyev nods to all my questions. "A regular Hercules the way my two useless men described him, though I figured they were just making most of that up to explain how one man could beat both of them up."

"Can we speak to these men?" Schmitt asks. "Get a clear description of the man they saw?"

The man's dark eyes—same eyes as his daughters—go so cold I clearly see the endless winter of his soul. "They no longer work for me."

I have no doubt they no longer work for anyone. Maybe they'll find their bodies washed up by the river Spree come Spring or maybe no one will ever see them again.

"Did your daughter ever work as an illegal prostitute?" I ask.

"No!" the man yells, banging both his fists against the table. "How dare you ask that? Who are you anyway, what's your name?"

He asks in a way that makes me think my body might or might not be washed up by the river come spring.

"I'm Special Investigator Mark Novak," I tell him. "I work for the US Military."

The cold look in the man's eyes goes from dangerous to deadly. "Yes, the man who took my daughter was American. Most likely a soldier. Are you here to cover up for him?"

It's not really a question, it's a statement, and I doubt anything I say will convince him otherwise. "No, I am here to help find your daughter's killer, whoever he is. This man she was with is definitely a suspect, one we'd like to find as soon as possible, so a description of him and where he was last seen would be very helpful."

"I'll get you a description," the man says, pulling out his phone and dialing someone on his speed dial. Then he proceeds to issue instructions in hurried Russian, which I have trouble following. I only have a middling knowledge of Russian, but I can understand enough to know he's telling someone to go do something, and I hope I was wrong about the two men ending up in the river.

"You will get your description," Alexeyev says. "My men were beaten very badly while trying to save my daughter. Now I would like to go make the identification. Perhaps all of this is not even necessary."

The longing in his voice is overwhelming, and I hope nothing to kill it is showing on my face. He stands up laboriously as if he'd rather not, and his face is such a hard stone expressionless mask, I know he's about to go face his worst fear, no matter how much death he's already seen. I'm as sure as I can be that Pocahontas is his daughter Nadia.

"I'll see to it," Schmitt says and walks to the door. "Follow me."

I remain seated since I have no desire to witness this man's grief. What I've seen so far is already clouding my already clouded focus on this case. So much sadness, so much grief, such a twisted depraved maniac we're hunting.

"Another thing my men said," Alexeyev says, turning to me from the door. "My daughter called him

Russ or Ross. She apparently said to him, "Be careful, Russ, they're killers," while my men were fighting him."

My mind snaps straight to Eager Ross. He's tall and he's fairly muscular, but I doubt he could take two Russian Mafia thugs and live to tell about it.

"Thank you," I tell him and he grunts, nods and leaves.

As unlikely as it is that Ross has anything to do with this, I'm going to interview and investigate him, anyway. I'm not leaving any stone unturned, not when there's already so few to turn in this case.

17

MARK

Eva calls me just as I turn onto the avenue that will lead me to the gates of the base. I've been saving calling her as the last thing I do today, knowing I won't want to go anywhere else after I'm with her, in her cozy, if a little drafty, apartment. I've also been hoping she'll stay inside all day, waiting for me to stop by. It's the only way I know how to force her to do that. She doesn't take kindly to me questioning her independence, which she is fiercely protective of. Not that I mind. Not at all. I need my silences as much as she needs her freedom, and she doesn't call me out on those. Much. Just enough so I know she cares.

I'd like to get the interview with Eager Ross over with as soon as possible, but I hardly think twice before pulling over to the side of the road and answering her call.

"Are you OK?" I ask before saying anything else, the fear that she's not bubbling to the surface so strong the question just spills out.

"Yes, I'm fine, but you have to come to my apartment right away," she says. "I found someone who knows the man Selima was last with. You have to talk to her."

The adrenaline that starts pumping through my veins at what she said makes me see double instead of clearing my head. It's been a long day after an even longer night, and I don't know how much excitement I can still take today. I used to be able to go four days on a case before I collapse. Lately, as I started getting older, that's shortened to two, three if I really push it.

"Tall? Muscular? American?" I blurt out.

"Yes, yes, yes," she says. "And she can describe him to you. But you have to come now before she changes her mind."

"On my way," I say, pulling out without signaling and making a U-turn in the middle of the avenue to the sound of other cars' screeching brakes. By sheer luck, like I haven't yet experienced in this case, no one crashed into me.

I had planned on focusing solely on Pocahontas or Nadia Alexeyeva, but this lead is too good to pass up. If Eva's friend describes the same man as Alexeyev's thugs and Jakob, then we'll have the first solid lead since these murders started. One that might actually lead us to a man. The man we're looking for? It's much too early to hope for that. But I kind of am as I drive to

Eva's home through slowly, but thickly falling snow. The fat clouds that have been threatening snow all day finally broke, and I hope that's an omen signaling a break in the case as well. That would be right in keeping with Pocahontas'.backstory.

Not only did Eva's prostitute friend describe the man in detail, but she also provided a name. Russell Parcibal. An odd name like that should be easy to trace. Only thing is, I doubt she heard it right. When I questioned her, she said it could've been Percival, maybe, or something else altogether, but she was sure it started with a P.

The whole time I spoke to her, she looked everywhere but at me with fear-filled wide brown eyes, wiping her sweaty palms on the skirt of her fake leather dress, which couldn't have helped much. I did all I could to make her feel at ease, smiling as much as I could, talking as slowly as I could, but she kept glancing at Eva and the door, and I counted it a win that I got as much out of her as I did.

For almost an hour, she absolutely refused to go to the police station to work with a sketch artist, and nothing either Eva or I said changed her mind. In the end, I called Schmitt who agreed to bring a sketch artist to Eva's place. I could've gotten someone from the base to do it, but everything right now is pointing to an American soldier as the person we're looking for and rumors of that will spread like wildfire at the base. I don't want to give this man any forewarning that we're coming for him.

Schmitt arrived within half an hour of getting my call, bringing a female officer and a social worker along with the sketch artist. I tell Eva to stay inside with Mirela while she describes the man and motion for Schmitt to follow me out into the hall.

The stairs leading from one floor to the next in this building are interrupted by a small landing in the middle. A window stretches across it and the radiator under it is cold as ice. Outside, snow is coming down so thickly all I see is white.

"She says his name was Russell and she wasn't sure of the last name. Maybe Percival, maybe Parcibal, though I've never heard that word before," I tell Schmitt.

"Russell? That would be Russ for short," Schmitt muses. "Like the Russian said."

I nod. I suppose that takes Eager Ross off the hook since the physical description doesn't match him either. Ross has black hair and black eyes.

"Did the Russian come back with the men who saw this Russ?"

Schmitt shakes his head. "I doubt those men are still alive. Pity, now that we'll have a sketch. To show them."

I'd rather not dwell on that, so I won't.

"What new information did the woman who found the body provide?" I ask.

"She only saw two other people on her walk that

evening. An old man walking with a cane, and a tall athletic American jogger. He yelled aggressively at her dog to get away from him in English but ran away when she challenged him. She only got a very brief glance at his face, but she's sure he's got blue eyes and she's convinced herself that he was trying to keep her dog away from the riverbank even though the incident occurred about a kilometer away from the spot where she eventually found the body. At first, I was skeptical. There's plenty of joggers in that park. But the description she gave matches the others. She's working with a sketch artist too. Do you think we've found our man?"

Skepticism is thick in his voice as he asks it.

I shrug. "Maybe. Hopefully. He ticks a number of boxes on the list of traits we're looking for with this killer. Strong enough to carry a body up the stairs in the broken tower. Attractive enough to not arouse immediate suspicion in his victims. American. A soldier."

Schmitt nods pensively. "Sure, sure. But all these leads after six months of nothing. He was never this sloppy before."

I shrug. "He had to stage four bodies in a very short time so we'd find them all in one day. Maybe he just couldn't help being sloppy this time. Maybe he bit off more than he could chew."

I say the last in English since I don't know the equivalent phrase in German and chuckle, but my own words sound very thin to my own ears. For a methodical killer like the one we're hunting to get this sloppy in the middle of his spree is not something I'd have expected.

"You may be right," Schmitt says. "All these people who might have seen him are so random, so unexpected and unconnected that we're damn lucky we found them all. And we were very much overdue for some luck in this case."

"We sure were," I tell him.

"Oh, and the medical examiner called me before I left the station," he says. "Pocahontas—Nadia—she wasn't bled like the others. Her wrists and neck were cut and superglued together, but she wasn't bled. Maybe he's changing his MO."

"Or he was in a hurry," I say.

But that's yet another confirmation that the Pocahontas' murder is different from the rest. And if Eva's dangerous amateur sleuthing to find Mirela, who just happened to see another victim with a guy who matches all the other descriptions, is taken out of the picture, that case is also the only one that has any witnesses. An accident or design. It sure looks a lot like the latter. But if The Fairytale Killer is sending us a message, I'm not getting it. Yet. I hope.

18

EVA

I spoke to the social worker in the living room the entire time Mirela was describing the guy she saw to the sketch artist in the kitchen. The gist of it was that, yes, they can set her up in a safe house, but they can't make her stay there against her will. Mark and the short black-haired detective came in about halfway through my conversation and went directly into the kitchen. The look of quiet longing Mark gave me on his way there, cut right to my heart and I missed a whole section of what the social worker was saying just then.

He came back in a couple of minutes later and asked for a word with me. In private. In the bedroom, which is still as messy as it was the morning he got that first call, and still smells of him, of us, of the reunion sex. It seems like it belongs in another life now.

Though, to be honest, we were living on borrowed time then, enjoying a reprieve we both knew was temporary. We just pretended it wasn't.

What I feel for him as I close the bedroom door behind us and face him is like nothing I've ever felt for another person. It's a mixture of love and devotion, care, and tenderness, along with the butterflies of desire all rolled into more than the sum of its parts. To say I love him doesn't even come close to describing how I really feel.

He pulls me into a loose embrace, his hands on my lower back. He needs a shave and sleep. His whole face is greyish with tiredness, even the bags under his bloodshot eyes. But his eyes are alert and alive with all those things I feel for him and more. He has the most expressive eyes I've ever seen on an adult, usually, such pure mirth and innocence are only reserved for children. I'm amazed he was able to retain that after all he's seen. I try to, but I know my eyes betray my bitterness and frustration at the world and what I've seen of it.

"It's not safe for you out on the streets, especially back alleys like the ones where you found Mirela," he says slowly, hesitatingly. He's afraid I'll get mad. And any other time, I probably would.

I smile instead and run my hand down his cheeks, the stubble prickling my palm.

"I can take care of myself," I say. "And I'm not really his target age or occupation."

He shakes his head slowly like he's considering

what to say. "We don't know enough about this guy to be sure of anything. I'd rather you stayed safe."

"And I'd rather you did too, Mark, but you've got a job to do and so do I. This monster killed a friend of mine and I'll do what I can to get him caught."

He gives me a sad little half-smile, his eyes full of worry he can do nothing about. Then he pulls me into a tighter embrace, holding me so hard it's hard to breathe for a moment. I hold him just as tightly. Just holding him is rejuvenating, and as we break apart, I have no doubt it was the same for him. Some color has returned to his cheeks and there are sparks in his eyes that weren't there before.

"I'll be careful," I promise him. "But you be careful too. Starting with getting some sleep. Stay here with me tonight, after they leave."

He was going to tell me he can't, I could see it in his eyes, but it was interrupted by shouting and cursing from the kitchen. Mirela is refusing to go with them. She's threatening to jump out the window if they don't let her walk out alone. He let's go of me.

"She's a witness, and she is very likely in danger," Mark says. "Once this guy realizes how much she knows, he will eliminate her. That much I can say for certain. He's too methodical and precise to leave loose ends he knows about."

"I know," I say. "But I doubt she'll listen to me."

I open the bedroom door just as the front door slams behind Mirela, so I guess we'll never know.

Detective Schmitt shrugs at Mark, holding his

hands out, palms out. "We have nothing to hold her on. We can put a tail on her, that's all we can do."

"I say do it," Mark says and Schmitt issues the instructions to the female officer who leaves right away. The social worker leaves with her, while the sketch artist is standing by the door, holding a large briefcase under one arm and an easel under the other. I never got to see the man Mirela described and I regret that now. But very likely the sketch will be all over the media, print, and broadcast, very soon. I'll probably get sent a copy.

"Do you want to come back to the station and interview the dog walker?" Schmitt asks Mark.

Mark nods. "Yes, I'll meet you there."

Schmitt leaves, ushering the sketch artist out before him.

"I was serious, Mark, you need rest," I tell him. "You look about ready to collapse."

He chuckles. "I'm not as far gone as that. But I'll come right back here once I'm done at the station, I promise. Though it's very important that we work this case while the trail is still hot."

There's no use arguing, he'll do what he needs to do just as I do what I need to do. Allowing each other that is the foundation of our relationship, and the fact that we can do that for each other is very likely the main reason we're still together. That and the fact that I love him the way I've never loved any other man. Like family. I love him like family.

MARK

I didn't find out much more than Schmitt did from the dog walker who found Pocahontas' body, and she was quite agitated at having to wait around the station for six hours by the time I finally got to her. She took her time looking at the composite sketch the artist made on Mirela's instructions, and after about twenty minutes confirmed she is as sure as she can be that it's the same man she saw in the park. By then, the light grey walls of the station were flickering before my eyes and I no longer trusted my judgment on anything, because of my tiredness, which went right past the sluggish phase into the stage where my whole body prickles like my blood is on fire.

But we still had to decide what to do with the sketch.

The man Mirela described has a narrow forehead and prominent brows under thick eyebrows, which she says are darker than his hair, which is long enough for waves of it to fall into his eyes. The eyes are deep-set, big, and spaced quite far apart. Bright blue, according to Mirela. He also has a straight nose, not too small and not too big, nicely-shaped lips, and a prominent jaw with just a hint of a cleft in his chin. The more I look at the picture, the more I start to believe that Mirela really liked the look of this guy and she described him more favorably than she would have if that wasn't the case. He's clearly a good looking guy, which would make sense since his victims seem to not only go with him willingly, but enjoy spending time with him. But for everything on his face to be this symmetrically and perfectly shaped, he'd have to be a model, not a soldier.

By midnight, when even Schmitt was having trouble keeping his eyes open and finishing his sentences, we decided to get a couple hours' rest. First thing in the morning, I'm taking a copy of the sketch to Marisa at CID's forensic lab and having her check it against service photos. And Schmitt will dispatch officers to canvas all the known prostitution spots and show the photo around. Only if all that leads nowhere will we go public with the image. Until then, it's best that this guy doesn't know we're coming for him.

Eva's hair is a frizzy mess around her head and she can barely keep her eyes open as she leads me to the bedroom, where she's asleep again by the time I undress, take a quick shower and get in bed with her. The sheets are wonderfully warm from her body heat, and I barely muster the energy to pull her into my arms before drifting off to sleep. It's easy not to worry or fret when I'm with Eva. That's how I know she's a keeper.

19

MARK

When I woke up, snow was still coming down in clumps as big as my fist, making it seem lighter outside than my six AM alarm clock suggested. Eva slept right through the alarm clock I set the night before, but she was sitting up in bed rubbing sleep from her eyes when I emerged from the shower cleanly shaven.

She looked young and kind of lost as she tried to wake up enough to speak. But I saw all that as through a pane of thick, not very clear glass that somehow sprouted in my mind during the night. I recognize it as detachment, and it always happens when I'm overwhelmed. A defense mechanism, which I'm not sure is a good response, but at least it allows me to view things more clearly.

"I'm going to the office," I tell her. "You should get some more sleep."

I walk over to the ancient mahogany dresser by the window. It's shiny like it's brand new, but that's just good craftsmanship and matches the massive king-sized bed and two closets that are overflowing with Eva's clothes. I have two drawers in the dresser for mine. We haven't discussed moving in together yet, but she did let me have that space for a change of clothes and I have a whole set of toiletries neatly stacked in a small area to the left of the sink in the bathroom. I've gotten further in some of my past relationships, but it never felt as natural as this does.

She stretches and gets up, the comforter sliding off her and landing on the floor where she leaves it. I love how free she is in everything she does. It lets me be free around her.

"I thought I'd try to find Mirela and convince her to go to a safe house," she says, looking around the room until she locates her lavender cardigan under a pile of clothes on the armchair between the two huge closets. "Because she's not safe on the streets anymore, is she? Not after you release the sketch to the media. Not if the man she described is this killer."

She's talking fast, trying to convince me, trying to justify it, because she's clearly reading the tightness that formed in my chest on hearing that plan off my face. She walks over, wrapped in her cardigan.

"It's the middle of the day," she says. "I'll be safe."

I brush a lock of her hair that's fallen over her bright, summer sky eyes back behind her ear. "We won't be releasing the sketch yet. But you have to do this, don't you?"

She gives me a look that's so full of gratitude and love that some of it filters through the glass pane in my mind. "Yes."

I hug her close then, kiss her because it's the only thing I want to do, for the rest of the day, for the rest of the decade, for the rest of my life.

But there's no time for that now.

"Just be careful, all right? Promise me." I say as I break away.

"I always am," she says, no edge in her voice.

Much too soon I'm dressed and we're saying goodbye by the door. And it's hard walking out into the chilly, snowy street after the warmth of her.

The thick curtain of snow masked most of the sound on my drive to the base, as though wrapping everything in cotton, giving a very false sense that everything is just fine. It's not. The CID building rose as drab and uniform as ever behind that curtain, and the inside was still very quiet and subdued. Until I reached the corridor leading to the forensics lab. There, the bustle could be heard before I even reached the main room.

In there, I was greeted by ten of the crime techs, including Ross, who I still want to talk to at some point, and Blackman. He was sitting in the exact spot where I left him yesterday, in the middle of one of the longer sides of the table, and if he didn't look rested, his dark eyes alert, I'd think he hadn't moved.

"Any new developments?" I ask the room at large, but mostly him.

The crime scene photos we received in the mail had been replaced by the ones our techs had taken, and he's got a number of other documents arranged all around them. As far as I can tell from a distance, he has it all arranged by case, with a picture on top, then the documents and reports related to it cascading down. It seems like a lot of stuff, but I bet nothing we'll be able to follow anywhere. That's how it was on the first two cases.

"Our German colleagues have sent us many samples they collected from the bodies and surrounding area and we've been analyzing them all night," Eager Ross answers. "So far it's been determined that the superglue used to close the incisions is the same as before, the DNA found matches across all the cases and the crystal shoe is made using an ancient glass blow method used only in the Veneto region of Italy. We'll be trying to trace the purchase to a specific shop today as soon as they open for business."

I nod.

"And the Germans found a DNA sample under the fingernails of one of the victims, which does not match the other DNA collected," Blackman says and Eager Ross grimaces. I can see why. He really should've led with that information, but he's nothing if not organized in his reports. The problem is, it's some sort of organization only he understands and usually starts with the least important bits first.

"Run it through our database to see if we come up with a match," I say.

Several heads turn to me, including the lab boss'. She clears her throat. "You mean the external databases we have access to?"

I shake my head. "No, I mean the database of military employees."

She winces, and several of them exchange glances, wondering if I'm once again overstepping my bounds. I'm not ready to reveal what we'd found last night to everyone. I'll keep it on a need to know basis until we find the man Mirela described.

"It's warranted," I add since she looks like she might start arguing.

She nods and tells Ross to do it.

I finally take off my coat, which I clean forgot to do as I entered, and hang it over a vacant seat around the table.

"I have decided that the best course of action is to focus on the Pocahontas victim. She doesn't fit with the others. Her name is Nadia Alexeyeva, and she is, was, the daughter of a big-time Russian mafia lord, who heads a syndicate of mob families here in Berlin. She wasn't an illegal prostitute at any time. And what is even more interesting is that of all the victims so far, she was not bled."

"But she had the super glued cuts," Ross interjects as I pause for breath. I wish he hadn't.

"Yes, she was cut in the same places as the others, but these cuts were not used to empty her body of blood," I answer.

"I believe this killer is trying to send us a message through this victim," I continue. "And we were also able to locate a witness of sorts."

Several of them gasp as I reveal this, Blackman included.

"It's only a very vague description, so not enough to pin hope on just yet," I say, not liking the need to deceive them like this, but secrecy is necessary right now. "But the Russian mobster is also looking for two of his men who might have seen this same person with his daughter shortly before she died."

Blackman nods and picks up one of the documents related to Pocahontas. "I did wonder about this one and thought it'd be best to look into her more closely. She doesn't fit with the others because she's not a fairytale princess like the others. And her character is based on a real historical figure."

Somehow, hearing him, a legend among CID investigators, and an expert on serial killers confirm my thinking on this fills me with something very similar to pride.

"I'd like one of you to prepare a report on Pocahontas as soon as possible. Everything you can dig up," I say.

"Wanda, would you," the lab head says, and timid Wanda nods while looking down at the floor.

"Email it to me by this evening, or as soon as you

have it," I tell her and she nods and leaves for one of the offices to our left.

Marisa is in her office too, her chair pushed back from the wall of computers so she can follow our conversation better.

"All right, that's it for now," I tell them. "If you find anything or get a DNA match, let me know right away."

They all nod or voice their assent then go back to doing what they were doing before I interrupted them.

"Come with me," I tell Blackman, avoiding Ross' gaze. The younger man clearly wants to ask me something, but it can wait. It's time to do what I came here to do.

I lead Blackman into Marisa's office and close the door behind us. She's looking at me with one eyebrow raised as I turn back to her. Blackman's gaze is equally questioning, but in his case, it's all in the eyes and not in the actual expression on his face.

"We have a sketch of a possible suspect," I tell them, seeing no reason to beat around the bush. "And a general description that strongly indicates he's US Military."

"You have been productive," Blackman says appreciatively. "This is all from the witness you found at the Pocahontas crime scene?"

I shake my head. "No, the witness who gave the description is tied to one of the other cases. Sleeping Beauty, to be exact. She was also able to provide us with a name. Or part of a name."

Blackman keeps nodding and I don't think he's

aware of it. Marisa looks impressed and determined like she usually does.

"The first name is Russell, she was sure of that, but I fear she might have gotten the last name wrong," I say.

"What is it?" Blackman asks just as I was about to say it.

"She's says something like Parcibal, but supposes it could also be Percival," I say and pull my phone from my pocket, turning to Marisa. "I'm sending you the sketch now. Then I'd like you to run it against the database and see if any of our personnel looks like it."

She nods, grabbing her mouse and looking at the screen. A few moments later, the printer to her side whirs, and a moment later it spits out the composite sketch.

Marisa picks it up. "He's a good looking guy. But also very generic looking. It could pose a problem. I could find too many matches."

She's not wrong, and I was afraid of that. "Narrow it down to men between twenty-five and thirty and first name Russell," I say. "Then widen the search if you get no hits."

"OK, will do," she says, somehow managing to perfectly convey the unspoken, sarcastic, *Yes, thank you, I know what I'm doing.*

Blackman reaches for the sketch and studies it, his lips a thin pink line, but his eyes bright. "Did the witness mention any distinguishing marks or tattoos? I am sure the man whose back is visible in the photos has a tattoo on his neck. Wings it looks like, or perhaps feathers."

I shake my head. "She only saw him briefly twice and both times he was dressed in a large black down jacket against the cold. She only saw his face clearly. Those were her words."

"Can you print me off a copy of the sketch too," Blackman asks Marisa.

"This information can't leave this room yet," I tell them sternly. "It might be an active duty military member we're searching for and I want to prevent word that we're looking to reaching him before we find him. So do not share this information with anyone, is that clear?"

I spoke to Marisa who nods curtly. "Yes, sir."

I hope Blackman understood that I meant him too. He folds up his copy of the sketch and puts it in his pocket like maybe he has before following me out of the office.

"Would you like to accompany me out in the field today?" I ask him as he closes the door to Marisa's office behind him.

He shakes his head. "Not yet. I wish to go over all the evidence and reports here first. And I'd like to oversee the database searching, both for the DNA and this man." He pats the pocket where he put the sketch. "It's how I work best. And I think you're right about keeping these findings under wraps for the time being. At least until we speak to this man."

I'm relieved by that. I have no patience for sifting through the reports or sitting still for that matter.

"Very good job, by the way, Major," he tells me. "I couldn't have narrowed this one down any better."

I'm sure he could've, but somehow I don't feel patronized at all. I feel vaguely proud at being praised by him. It's that radio announcer voice of his, I decide, it makes everything he says sound important and permanent.

"Thank you," I say. "I'm just glad we're finally making some inroads into this case."

He nods slowly. "Yes, it's hard to crack. But you're on the right track."

But as I leave the lab, I'm not so sure we are. More and more, it all seems too easy the way it's falling into our laps after months and months of it being impossible to find a single solid lead. But I also recognize the voice telling me that. It's the voice of fear and pessimism. The one that'll never believe we caught the killer, even after I do.

20

MARK

Two days of searching revealed absolutely nothing new. Eva had been unable to locate Mirela anywhere, the Russian hadn't been in contact, Marisa's search for active-duty members in the area matching the sketch and description yielded over a thousand hits on the first round, and she's still working on narrowing that down to a manageable number. I suggested she focus only on disgruntled personnel now, so hopefully, she'll have someone for me to check out soon. The DNA search is still ongoing, but no hits yet. None of the glassmakers in the Venice region have any recollection of creating glass slippers, but they all said they would check their files. None got back to us yet.

I spent most of my time on the streets, helping canvas the areas where the victims were most likely taken from, but the merry snowfall turned to freezing cold, driving everyone into hiding. The snow stuck to the sidewalks and roads, turned to ice now, as cold as these damn leads have turned. After that short burst of sunshine, everything turned to ice again.

The only complete report I've received was Wanda's Pocahontas write-up and even that held nothing that shone any kind of light in any new direction. Pocahontas was a Native American woman born in 1596. Her father was Powhatan, the paramount chief of an alliance of about thirty chiefdoms in Tidewater, Virginia. She was captured by Colonialists is 1613, converted to Christianity during her captivity, and christened Rebecca. She died of unknown causes when she was just twenty-one-years-old and was buried in England, the exact location of her grave unknown.

I showed the report to Eva when we had dinner last night, but nothing jumped out at her either.

She called me an hour ago, just as I was pulling in through the military base gates, asking if I want to have dinner again. I do. But I can't. I have a meeting with Blackman and then I'm spending the rest of the night reviewing what the team here has found. Maybe my presence will make it move faster, though I don't doubt that every one of them is doing their best.

And I'll just sleep in my office, I also tell her, sitting in my car in the parking lot in front of the HQ building, looking at its many identical windows, many of which are dark. It's nearly eight PM, so most of the people who work there have already gone home. The lab, where I know at least fifty people are working at any given time has no windows since it's in the basement, but I bet all those lights are on right now.

Walking into the building feels like entering a mausoleum, the thick walls radiating cold and damp. Nothing's going to be solved in this building, I know it. But there's nothing to find in the freezing streets of Berlin either. I wish the Russian would at least give us the exact location of where that fight his men described happened so we can try and find a fresh lead from there, but so far all attempts to contact him have been a bust.

Blackman was assigned an office upstairs, but he spends all his time down in the lab and that's where he wants to meet me. I find him in one of the glass-walled offices off the main room, which is empty. Marisa is shut away in her own office, barely visible behind her wall of computers.

Blackman has put two of the desks in the center of the room to make one long table and has all sorts of reports and photos and documents arranged on it in no order than I can decipher.

"You wanted to speak to me?" I say when he doesn't notice me walk in, since his back is turned to the main room.

"Ah, yes, Novak," he says as he turns, fixing the round glasses which had slid almost to the tip of his narrow nose. He catches sight of his reflection in the glass walls behind me and starts smoothing down his short hair. I bet he ruffled it running his hands through his hair.

I walk over to the desk.

"I've been immersing myself in the work of this killer," he says. "And I have a hard time imagining he's as young as the man in the sketch. All these scenes, they took so much planning and were all executed so meticulously, both those things speak to an older person. Then there's the sophistication of the presentation. The bodies are arranged like works of art, if you will. This is not the work of someone just starting out. This took years and years of planning and figuring out. In all my studies I've come across two, maybe three similar murderers, and none of those operated in this kind of scope."

I nod like I'm interested, but actually I'm just trying hard not to say what I'm really thinking. Namely, that he's spent too much time with his books and his studies and not enough time out in the field these past fifteen years since he retired from CID.

"There is an element of childishness to these murders, though," I say. "Fairy princesses, cartoon characters, the intimate way in which he knows them and is able to recreate them."

Blackman reaches over and picks up a piece of paper. "Never in my career or my studies did I ever come across a serial killer with this level of sophistication on his first crime. Whichever one of the first two were his first, they were both staged as perfectly as the last four. I took the liberty of having Sargent Smith-Marisa-look up unsolved crimes similar to these in the area." He holds out the paper for me to take. "She found two. Young women, students, raped and killed with a strong mixture of sleeping pills, their bodies left in a forest as though they were just sleeping. These happened in 2007, about one year before the first princess was found."

I take the paper and scan it, the words dancing before my eyes. He could be onto something.

"I'll tell Detective Schmitt. They can start by checking the DNA from these cases against that found in ours," I say.

"That's a good start," Blackman says and pulls the photos of both Cinderellas and Sleeping Beauties closer, laying them side by side. "Then there's another thing that worries me. He's creating several scenes with the same main character. Are we to assume he's planning on retelling each of these fairytales in bodies? I think he might be."

"I'm afraid he is too," I say, voicing that fear for the first time since it gripped me when I saw Cinderella and Sleeping Beauty for the second time. "But he's already overreaching and getting sloppy. We have to focus on following the breadcrumbs he's accidentally leaving behind and do it fast. Then we have a chance of catching him."

"He's not sloppy," Blackman says, his eyes laser-focused on mine, a typical reaction of an older man who's one-hundred percent sure he's right to being disagreed with. I didn't come here to butt heads with him and I'm not sure how to diffuse it, since my mind's too full of what I should be doing instead of this.

Like checking on DNA results, seeing if Marisa has had any luck...

"I think I found something, Sir...Sirs," she says behind my back as though summoned by my thought.

I turn to find her clutching a relatively thick manila file and poking just her head through the door.

"Come in," I tell her. "What is it?"

She enters, closing the door slowly. "Well, I did as you suggested and narrowed the search by discharged personnel, non-active duty members that is, and ones that might have a grudge."

I nod impatiently for her to get on with it.

"I found these five guys," she says, opening her folder with shaking hands and almost dropping the entire contents. "None of them are named Russell though, but there's a Robert. Robert Greaves. And all of them were discharged dishonorably while serving here, this Robert most recently. About two years ago, following an incident where he was accused of rape by a cafe waitress Prenzlauer Berg."

"I remember the case," I say, taking the folder from her. It was going on right about the time I moved here, and while I wasn't involved with it directly, I had heard of it. "He refused transfer back to the states, didn't he?"

"Yes," she says while I'm still scanning the write up on him she compiled.

His service photo shows a guy with vacant blue eyes, closely cropped blonde hair and a slightly crooked nose, like it'd been broken in the distant past and healed well. This guy isn't as strikingly handsome as the guy in the sketch, but Mirela most likely exaggerated his features. This could be our guy.

"Do you have any last known addresses for these men?"

She shakes her head. "All of them except Greaves were transported stateside since all except him were officially discharged there. What also struck me is that, in reading his file, it seems he was a model soldier until he transferred to Berlin in 2004. Then he began making trouble. But I was thinking, the German police might have something on him. If he's a rapist, I mean." She looks up at me hopefully.

I nod. "I'll check. Good work. But keep digging, and let me know as soon as you find anything."

She assures me she will and leaves.

"This one would fit your rapist theory as well," I say to Blackman once she's gone, offering him the file. "I'm going to start with him."

Blackman studies it, humming very quietly as he does. "Maybe," he finally says. "He does look a lot like the sketch. But his file tells me he's completely disorganized. He has several citations for insubordination and disorderly conduct prior to his discharge. I find it hard to believe he could be the mind behind these murders."

"I'll find him and we'll see," I say, as courteously as I can.

There's a time and place for scholarly musings and this isn't it. Although, as I take the file and leave him, I know that a large part of my agitation with him is stemming from the fact that I think he's right. I'm about to go grasp at yet another very short straw, but I'm also convinced that we won't find this guy by staying in the lab following only the evidence he wants us to find. The only way we'll catch him is by following the mistakes he makes.

I had three missed calls from Schmitt when I took out my phone to call him on my way out of the lab. Everything else can wait for now, while we focus on tracking down this Robert Greaves.

"About time," Schmitt snaps as he picks up. "The Russian is coming down to the station with one of the men who saw our guy, Russell. He should be here soon, so I suggest you hurry if you want to speak to him."

I'm in the elevator and pump the button for Lobby as if that's going to make it rise any faster. "I'm on my way. Don't let them leave until I get there."

"You got something?" Schmitt asks, an uncharacteristic tone of excitement in his otherwise clipped voice.

"Yes, I think I do," I say and hang up since this isn't something I can discuss while rushing down the hall of HQ to the exit.

Outside, I waste even more time scraping ice off my windshield, but I kind of, sort of feel my frozen fingers again by the time I reach the police station. A large, loud group of tourists, British soccer fans by the look of them, is crowded around the reception desk and I have

THE FAIRYTALE KILLER

to stand by the double doors leading upstairs, trying to get the attention of one of the officers behind the reception desk. I finally catch the eye of a female officer who was working the night the Russian first came here and wave at her to let me in. As I slip in, I spot a dwarf, possibly also the same one as the other night, rushing towards me though I could be wrong about that.

I never realized just how slow elevators in this building were, but eventually, after what feels like an eternity, it finally opens on the third floor. The hallway here is narrow and separated from the office space by a thin wall of metal and mottled glass. The room where we interviewed the Russian the first time is at the end of this hallway to the left of the elevators and I head there and knock just in case I'm wrong about them being there. Schmitt's clipped, "Come in," tells me I'm not.

Inside, Schmitt and the Russian Alexeyev are both sitting, Schmitt at the head of the oval table dominating the room and Alexeyev to his right. The chairs on the right side of the table have been pushed away to make room for a man in a wheelchair. A thick, padded bandage is wrapped around his head and his left eye, his right arm is in a sling, and his leg is in a cast that comes up to his hip. He doesn't even notice me come in, his one clear blue eye open, but I doubt he sees anything much with it. I hope he's going to be able to at least see the photo I want to show him.

I see Schmitt has already started the interview since

the sketch is laying on the table in front of the injured man.

"He says this sketch looks like the man who took Nadia," Schmitt says. But I'm still not convinced this man sees much or how much is left of his memory.

I take a chair and sit across from him so our eyes are level. "Can you tell me where this incident occurred?" I ask.

The expression in the man's eyes barely changes, but his one good eye does flicker in Alexeyev's direction.

"His German is very poor," Alexeyev says. "I will translate."

I shake my head and repeat the question in Russian. It's similar to my grandparents' native Slovenian, and that's all I spoke when with them. That and Italian. I was fluent in three languages before I even started school, which might be why learning new languages comes so easily to me. It's definitely a skill that comes in handy working in Europe.

The man's eyes flicker to Alexeyev again, who gives him a curt nod. The man starts speaking then, describing an abandoned industrial zone at the edge of the Friedrichshain district, and, more specifically, an abandoned bottling plant, where junkies and other squatters make their home. His speech is slurred, and the words came in fits and starts, but he sounds coherent enough. Could be he isn't brain damaged from his injuries, but only on very strong pain medication. He certainly gave us enough information to find the abandoned plant and start searching for the guy there.

I open the folder I'm carrying, pull out the photo of Robert Greaves and show it to the witness. "Is this the man you fought?"

He squints at the photo with his good eye. "It could be. Yes…yes, I think it is."

"You think it is or it is?" Alexeyev barks at the man. Both Schmitt and I give him a nearly identical warning look, but he's not fazed at all and just keeps glaring at his man.

"Yes. It is. But his eyes aren't as crazy as they were that night. The man's eyes glowed with crazy," the guy elaborates speaking as cohesively as I've yet heard him, which tells me he's not lying. "His hair was longer too. Blond. Hanging down past his eyes."

"Robert Greaves, is that his name?" Alexeyev says after glancing at the file which I'm holding open, with my finger marking the spot I took the photo from. Dumb.

I close the file and look at him. "I can't answer this question at this time."

"Have you found him yet?" Alexeyev asks, as though I haven't spoken at all.

"This is an ongoing investigation, I can't give you that information."

Schmitt is glancing from me to him with ever-growing annoyance on his face.

"What's going on?" he asks. "Did he ID the guy?"

"Yes," I say and leave it at that since I don't want to go into any more detail in front of Alexeyev.

"I think we're done here," I tell Alexeyev in German. "But please stay reachable. We might need your man to come back in soon to ID the man in person."

Alexeyev stands up and cracks a lopsided grin. "I'll find this man for you," he tells me in Russian.

"Alive," I answer. "He needs to be alive."

There's no way to tell what he's thinking. His eyes are as expressionless as a concrete wall. I keep looking at him waiting for an answer though. Finally, he inclines his head just a touch. I might have messed up letting him see the name of our person of interest, but maybe it'll turn out for the best. We need all the help we can get tracking him down. So long as he delivers him to us alive, I'll consider it a job well done.

Schmitt walks them to the elevator and once he returns, I tell him all I found out at the base. In the retelling, it becomes painfully obvious how little that was. But half an hour later, I'm arranging for the DNA evidence to be transferred, under guard, to the forensic lab at the base. They're also including the print they found on one of the photos sent to the station since they haven't been able to find a match in any of the databases they have access to so far.

Very little is actually happening, but I still feel like we're finally rushing forward on this case. Although I have to admit that the ID we got from the Russian thug is very shaky. And how could it not be? The guy we're looking for looks like every third man in Germany.

And an American accent is easy enough to fake if one is determined enough.

Schmitt and I rode to Greaves' last known address in the Prenzlauer Berg district, but that entire building had been demolished, along with all the other buildings on the block. The skeletons of new ones have already gone up. Staring into the dark hull of apartments that will eventually probably be very modern, chipped away at the elation of finally moving ahead on this case I felt just hours ago. I suspected it was just the first of many disappointments. I wasn't wrong.

Next, we joined the officers who were canvassing the bottling plant where Nadia was last seen in the company of a blond man. As I suspected it is a bustling squat, located about five kilometers east of the building Greaves used to occupy. So I was glad I insisted that only plain-clothes officers were sent to search it and find out if any of the residents know who the blond man with Nadia was.

Places such as that had once started much closer to the city center, but even in the three years since I lived here, they've been moved back to the edges. Gentrification is occurring at light speed here, which is something Eva complains about a lot. She's lived in this city for about six years now, and already it's not the same as it was, according to her.

Some abandoned factories in this district have

already been turned into concert halls and galleries, which is slowly but surely putting Berlin on the map as a cultural capital of Europe.

But the bottling plant is still a derelict, crumbling ruin. It has a large, low rectangular building, spanning a whole city block. Its main room still contained some of the heavy machinery once used here, most of it rusted beyond recognition. The plant also had a large warehouse area. Several fires burned in that room, some in metal barrels, some on the concrete floor, filling the space with thick smoke. Most of the residents fled when we arrived, and the ones we were able to catch, didn't want to talk to us. Eventually, they were hauled off to jail for the night, with the hope that they'll be more willing to cooperate once they're warm and fed. And starting to feel the pangs of withdrawal.

The last of them was taken away at four in the morning, and as much as I wanted to go sleep at Eva's, I went to my own apartment instead.

It's a lot more modern than Eva's and much warmer. Yet colder in a way that can't really be described, only felt, and it all stems from her absence. Thinking about it would've kept me from sleeping had I not been so dead tired. But the last thing I do remember thinking is that Eva and I should start giving some serious thought to moving in together. Which is another thing that would've kept me awake in all my previous relationships. But since it's Eva, it worked better than a sleeping pill.

21

EVA

During the night, an ice flower formed in the corner of the living room window where the two panes of glass don't sit quite flush with the window's white wooden frame. It's prettier than any that have formed there in the past, larger than the span of my hand, almost perfectly round yet created of such intricate, complicated, and gorgeous geometric patterns I've just been staring at it, trying to see it all. Each pattern is similar, but not exactly the same. I should be writing. And part of the reason I'm not is that, at this point, with the police so sparse with the details about the murders they're releasing, all I've been able to write is just a rehashing of what everyone else is printing.

I've started outlining an article about how the enhanced police presence on the streets is letting the illegal immigrants starve even worse than they were before. That led me to research the scope and level of illegal immigration in Berlin, and Germany as a whole, and into what is being done about it. It's not good. And it could be a lot better with not so much effort or money at all. But no news outlet is exactly clamoring for such human interest pieces. Not unless there's a flashy spin on it like I've been able to put in with my article on illegal prostitution in Berlin and its victims. Since The Fairytale Killer is targeting them, they finally had their voices heard…well, I spoke for them and they didn't exactly thank me for it. Maybe a follow-up article, urging the state to do more for them would do the trick…

My phone rings just as I loop back around to that thought and follow it to it's one and only conclusion. Namely, that no one cares right now. All they care about is this serial killer that emerged out of nowhere with a bang that's sent ripples across the world. One of the articles I'm working on now is for the New Delhi Times.

"I missed waking up next to you this morning," I say as I pick up the phone. It's Mark, and it's the complete truth.

He inhales sharply. "I had a hard time falling asleep without you."

"You should've come over."

"It was late, I didn't want to wake you," he says, regret thick in his voice so I know he's telling the truth.

My heart starts racing because of what I'm about to say.

"You should have your own key," I say kind of breathlessly and very quickly.

Given how independent he is and the sworn bachelor life he's led until now, coupled with how jittery men are about these kinds of big steps in relationships in general, my cheeks are flushed with nervousness and my heart is fluttering in my chest, as I wait for his reply. Wait to see how much damage I've done.

"I was actually thinking the same thing," he finally says, and I can hear the smile in his voice.

I let out the breath I've been holding. "Good, it's settled then. Meet me for dinner tonight and I'll have your key ready for you. Then you can come and go as you please."

"Seven-thirty? Mario's?"

"Yes, and yes," I say, throwing the blanket off my legs and standing up because I can't sit still any longer. I wish it was seven already, but it's not even ten AM.

Still, at least it gives me time to finish my work. There are still a ton of emails I haven't had time to check yet. Maybe one of them holds the spark that will take the articles I've yet to write in a whole new direction.

I was too antsy to work at home and kept glancing at the computer clock to see what time it was, and how much longer before I see Mark, my silliness driving me crazy. So I came here, to my favorite coffee shop slash library slash bookstore in this whole city. It's inside a narrow, pre-war, three-story family home. All the doors on the rooms have been removed and the ground floor houses a large coffee shop to the right of the entrance and a huge salon filled with comfy armchairs and sofas on the left. Almost all the walls are covered by floor to ceiling bookshelves filled with books in all shapes and sizes. Some are first editions of famous books, some are new paperbacks left behind by tourists, and the oldest book I've seen so far is a herbarium which I'm sure is from the 1800s, maybe older. Usually, I like to sit in the salon and watch people come and go, but today, I took my coffee to one of the tiny rooms on the third floor which is just big enough for two comfy, mismatched winged armchairs, a surprisingly sturdy dark wood table and two bookshelves filled to bursting. I'm sure this room used to be a servant's bedroom, but it's warm and cozy and small enough that no one ever comes and joins me here unless there are no other seats available, which rarely happens.

By three PM I've finished all four of the articles, two of which were due today and two which aren't due until tomorrow. I still have more than two hours before I'm meeting Mark, and I figure I'll just stay here, drink some more chamomile tea and finish digging through the rest of the emails. I only got through half my inbox before finding an email with photos of three newspaper articles about the women who were found raped and dead from sleeping pill overdoses a year or so ago. I remember the murders vividly because they made me afraid to go out after dark for the first time in my adult life. But the killings stopped though, and to the best of my knowledge, the killer was never caught. Yet, what if he's now back as The Fairytale Killer? That was the gist of the articles I just got done writing.

I start scrolling through my unread emails but don't have to go far. A day before the emails that inspired my articles today, I was sent another, even older article than the others. This one is titled, Growing up in the House of Horror. The date on the article is September 3, 1993, and there's a picture of two young children, a boy, and a girl, holding hands. They're both fair-haired, the girl's almost white hair falling across her down-turned face, so only her little nose and pursed lips are visible, while the boy clutching her hand is staring defiantly at the camera as though daring someone to come at him. The stark aggression in his eyes shoots through my chest and across the years. I've never seen such anger in a child's eyes. I've never even seen such anger in an adult's eyes.

The article itself is about how the brother saved his little sister, Rebecca P. After their mother died, shortly after Rebecca was born, the two had been systematically abused by their father, a US Army officer, in their Washington D.C. family home. The house itself is out of focus in the background of the photo, only its rough walls, and ornate two-sided dark brown or black door, and two windows above it visible. Lush green vines seem to be covering most of the facade of the house. A fairytale house. But a house of horror. According to the article, the children were both physically and sexually abused by their father, until the son shot him. He was eight years old. I have no idea what to do with this.

My phone rings, startling me. It's Christina, my editor at The Guardian.

"Hey, I got the emails you sent, but I'm still looking over them," I say as I pick up. "Though I'm ready to send you the article for tomorrow."

"I didn't send you any emails," she says, sounding confused. "I was just calling to see if you've found any new angle on this story. I hate to say it, but the stuff coming out about it is starting to get stale."

I check the sender of the email. I only glanced at it thinking I read "Christina" and "Guardian" but it is actually from ChildGuardian@freemail.com. The other articles came from the same address.

It's not the same email as the one I got the photo of Selima as Sleeping Beauty from, though that one was also sent from a disposable email service. That photo didn't come from anyone I know. My only contact at the police station was transferred to Munich late last year. I called him to check if he sent the photo to me, but he assured me he has no access to files related to The Fairytale Killer case.

Christina chuckles nervously. "I'm sorry for saying it. I feel like a total bitch now."

"What? No, that's not it," I say realizing she thinks she shocked me into silence. "Let me call you back. I might have something new, but I need to research it more before I'll know."

She tells me to get back to her quickly, and I promise I will then hang up, my heart still thumping in my throat.

I look at the boy in the photo again. I'm convinced I'm looking at The Fairytale Killer, even though I have no tangible reason to think that. But I mean to find the proof. All I have is his first name, Russell, and the initial of his last name. But I can find out more, I can find out everything, I just need to do some digging and make a few calls.

The cold, damp gust of wind straight off the icy Spree river takes my hood off as I walk out of the coffee shop at just before seven. Mario's where I'm meeting Mark is just a few doors down. A second ago, my cheeks were uncomfortably warm from sitting in the cozy, overheated former maid's bedroom in the coffeehouse, but now they freeze instantly in this arctic winter we're in the throes of. Only to redden and heat up again as the piercing, shining blue eyes of the most gorgeous guy I've seen in the last year or more lock on mine.

Around us, early evening darkness is making everything drab and two-dimensional. The bundled up strangers passing by in their drab, dark coats, and scarves wrapped tightly over their faces might as well be the backdrop of a stage set for all the life they're exhibiting. Not so the man with the bright blue eyes, though. His eyes are shining with the strength of the sun, which we haven't seen in this city for at least a week now. And this sun came out from behind the thick, dark grey clouds just for me. I'm blushing under the intensity and heat in that gaze, my stomach twisting in equal parts warning and excited, primal lust. Danger, flee! A part of my brain is saying. But why should I? He's just looking and I'm not going anywhere with him. I'm meeting my soon-to-be live-in boyfriend in less than ten minutes, so I'm just looking too.

It takes me a second to realize where that warning blaring part of the butterflies in my stomach is coming from. It's below zero outside, the wind carrying ice crystals it picked up on its way from the river to here, probably off the piles of snow that haven't melted because of the freezing temperatures. Yet this guy is wearing shorts that don't even cover his knees and a tank top. His neck is thick and tattooed, and his arms are bulky, muscular, and tattooed from the shoulder to the wrist in an intricate design I can't decipher in the darkness. They're the arms of a bad boy, the kind every girl secretly wishes to have wrapped around her at least once in her life. I had a bad boy boyfriend for a couple of weeks at university, and it was fun, but not something I've even considered since.

The black tank top he's wearing isn't skin tight, but the gusting wind has plastered it taut against his abs, which might actually be an eight pack rather than just a six-pack. His legs are muscular and shapely, the kind of legs one of those marble statues by Michelangelo would be jealous of. They're covered by tattoos too. A vicious-looking snake is baring its poisonous fangs there, peeking from beneath his leg hair as though hiding in the grass waiting for its unwary prey. Lifelike. Threatening.

Maybe his girlfriend just kicked him out. Maybe he got locked out of his apartment. Maybe he's insane. The gleam in his says so loud and clear, and yet I can't tear my eyes away from him.

"I heard you were looking for me," he says, his mouth stretching into a grin and revealing two sets of perfectly white, perfectly straight teeth. Not fangs. Not poisonous. Not right.

Do I flee back into the coffeehouse? Do I run down the street?

I have no idea what he's talking about.

"Nope. You got the wrong person," I say and smile, deciding that was most likely just a bad pick-up line, and it's best to play it off as such.

I start walking towards Mario's, but he falls in step beside me, even putting his arm around my shoulders. He's smiling, his eyes still shining, and his arm is much too heavy across my shoulders.

"Nope, I don't. Mirela said she told you all about me," he says in English—American English.

Piercing, sharp fear stabs through my chest right before my heart starts racing faster than it ever has. I duck from under his arm and try to run away, but he's got an iron grip on my upper arm.

"There, there," he says soothingly, his arm once again around my shoulders, but this time he's gripping me tight with his palm. "You'll make the perfect Snow White, with those big blue eyes and red lips. We'll just have to dye your hair first."

I open my mouth to scream, but he's ready for it and plants his lips over mine in a kiss. I taste the open grave on his, rot and death and dust and cold. Something sharp pricks the side of my neck and a split second later unnatural cold spreads down my neck as though he's injected me with liquid ice. Somehow, I have the presence of mind to take one of my phones from my jacket pocket and let it slip from my fingers to the ground. I have two. I can use the other to call for help.

The world is blurred and I can't feel my legs moving as he leads me towards the lights which are creating the prettiest bokeh I've ever seen.

22

MARK

A pressure headache's been building in my temples since I woke up this morning and it's not easing up, only getting worse despite the gallon of coffee I've drunk and the four or so aspirin I've taken. Now the smell of paint in the interview rooms at the station coupled with the dust of decades that permeates every room here and the body odor of our interviewees is making me nauseous on top of it. Most of the junkies and squatters we picked up last night probably haven't held a bar of soap yet this year, much less used it.

The ones who aren't refusing to speak to us have never seen a blond man at all to hear them tell it, and the ones that won't speak are either sitting in their chairs sullenly or demanding to see their lawyers. I was about to lose it with the next one that accused me of trampling all over his human rights, which is why I retreated to the small kitchen to get another cup of coffee, which is only making my nausea worse.

It's almost six PM and I can't wait to go meet Eva, though I'm not sure I'll be able to eat anything with her. And it won't be a long break either. I'll have to come right back here with the hope that Schmitt or one of the other detectives conducting the interviews managed to soften up one of the junkies to tell us something useful. One of the twenty we're holding has to have seen something. At least the damn fight with the Russian thugs.

My phone buzzes and I hope it's Eva, calling to see if we can meet earlier. Yes, we can.

But it's not Eva, it's Sargent Ross.

"I think I might have found something, Sir," he says in that breathless, excited way of speaking he has. It grates on my already frayed nerves more than it should.

"What is it?"

"The fingerprint on the photo sent to the German police came back a hit in our own database," he says.

"Who?" I ask, my headache disappearing like it never was as adrenaline surges through my veins.

"I can't access that information, it's marked confidential, it needs Level Five clearance," he says. "You need to come in, Sir."

"I'll be right there," I say and hang up. My heart's thumping with that special sort of excitement of finally catching the man I'm looking for, even though it's way too early to think it. But everything about this case has been weird and twisted, so I don't even question it.

I text Eva that something's come up and I won't be able to make dinner. I hate to do it, and it's only the thought of all the dinners we'll be able to share in peace after this fairytale monster is caught that makes me feel better.

As I exit the building, the dwarf is once again at reception, arguing with an officer behind the desk, yelling that he demands to see a detective right away. He's not going to have much luck getting one. Most of the available force has been routed to help conduct the interviews that will hopefully lead us to Greaves.

I keep the windows open as I drive to the base too fast. The surge of adrenaline at hearing Ross' news faded and left behind a full-on migraine, but I'm hoping the crisp cold air will take care of it. The evening gridlock is everywhere though, and the bright lights of the cars aren't doing my headache any good.

I broke several traffic laws, even going down a few one-way streets the wrong way, but it still took me almost an hour to reach the parking lot in front of HQ. There are only five cars still parked there and the streets and lanes around it, leading to other parts of the base, are completely empty, as though it's the middle of the night instead of seven PM. More than half the identical windows in the HQ building are still lit though, and that's the only sign that anyone's even here. That and a soldier is standing in the gloom by the main entrance, wearing a black cap and a wrapped in a fat black parka.

"Major Novak, sir," he says as I reach him, and it's only then I realize it's Ross.

"What are you doing out here, Sargent?" I ask. His cheeks and lips are pale white, only the tip of his nose red. He must've been standing out here for a while.

"I've been waiting for you," he says, confirming my suspicions. "I wanted to catch you before you came down to the lab."

I give him a questioning look.

"I'll explain in your office," he says and starts for the door.

I follow, hoping these theatrics aren't just for show, and, at the same time, that they are.

My office is on the second floor and smells of wood polish, leather, and dust that no one's wiped well for years. It also has that unused musky smell, with a hint of something sour underneath, a remnant of all the cigarettes that were smoked in here back when this office was used regularly. The entire building still reeks of cigarette smoke despite it being forbidden to smoke in here for over forty years.

I flip on the light and head straight for the window and open it.

When I turn back around Ross is standing with his back to the closed door.

"What's going on Sargent?" I ask.

"Well, it's like this," he says, moving farther into the room then coming to a stop again after taking two steps. "We weren't having any luck with matching the print in any of our databases, and I mentioned it to Major-General Thompson when he came down to see how the investigation was progressing."

"He came to the lab? That's not like him," I interject. But it makes some sense that he would. I haven't exactly been reporting to him regularly, hoping Blackman would do that since he was here all the time.

"I know," Ross says. "But he was there, Blackman at his side, and when it came to my turn to report I told him about the print. He suggested I check everything, even the sealed files."

"And what did you find?" I ask to speed him along.

"The print belongs to a two-star General, Sir," Ross mutters. "A Wallace Parcivall."

So Mirela had heard the name almost right.

"But all I got was the name and general information," Ross continues. "His record is sealed."

"Even Marisa didn't have the clearance?" I ask. "And you didn't think to go to Major-General Thompson with it?"

Something about Ross has bothered me since I met him. I can't tell if a very shrewd and calculated careerist is hiding behind his eager, diligent, and always helpful facade, or not. Sometimes I'm sure there is, other times I'm sure I'm wrong.

"Him and CoBlackman left after he visited the lab and haven't been back since," he says. "And I thought you should know first. You see, General Parcivall died in 1999. He had a heart attack during a NATO training mission in the UK."

"That part of his file isn't sealed?" I ask, confused.

He shakes his head. "His whole file is sealed. Marked Top Secret even. An internet search told me about how he died."

A man whose military record is marked Top Secret yet has internet search hits, leaving fingerprints on photos taken more than a decade after his death makes absolutely no sense.

The whirring of my computer as I turn it on and it powers up is keeping rhythm to the sinking feeling in my chest as I wonder if even I'll be able to access those files. Probably not without Thompson's approval. And files from the last century might not even be digitized yet. Which means they'll have to be sent from whatever archive they're kept in. Which means even more red tape to bypass since Top Secret files can't exactly be mailed overnight. The first solid lead we've had and I can't even follow it easily. Damn this twisted case!

The slow, incessant whirring of my computer had me seriously wanting to punch a hole through the screen by the time it finally came on fully. I pulled up my chair—a fake leather work chair that is a lot less comfortable than it looks—and motioned Ross to take a seat across from me. Accessing the database, or intranet, took another agonizingly long fifteen minutes and by the time my clearance wasn't enough to access the file my temper was flaring. And I'm usually very slow to anger.

I take a couple of deep breaths before rolling my chair away from the computer and facing Ross again.

"The Major-General will have to request the file," I tell him, my voice betraying every bit of how mad that makes me.

"Can you call him now?" Ross asks eagerly, while I'm still considering it.

Thompson is probably at home having dinner right now and most likely won't be able to get the ball rolling on this until tomorrow morning. But this isn't just any case, and this development isn't just any clue. It could hold the why of these gruesome killings, possibly even the who.

"Go back to the lab," I tell Ross. "I'll meet you there in a little while."

Only his face betrays that he's not happy about the order because he shoots up like an arrow and leaves promptly.

I lean back in my seat, pull out my phone, and dial Thompson's number. He picks up after the third ring, and the din in the background sounds like he's in a busy restaurant, meaning he's not alone. I explain the situation and what I need as succinctly as I can, aware that people could be hearing what I'm asking for.

"Put the request in writing and I'll approve it tomorrow morning," he says curtly and dismisses me.

The fact that he's outside and can't speak freely could be blamed for his haste to get off the phone, but it still leaves a sour feeling in my stomach. That last two aspirin I took and the fresh air seems to have finally taken care of my headache, but the nausea in my stomach is still annoyingly present.

Eva hasn't returned my text and worrying about her reasons why would only bring back my headache. So I call her instead. After fifteen rings and no reply, I finally admit defeat.

It's not like her to ignore my calls, even when she's angry at me. She's much more likely to tell me at length what I did to piss her off. But maybe this is different. I've never yet canceled a date at the last minute with no explanation after she'd offered to give me the keys to her apartment. If I start worrying about that, I'll lose the last little bit of drive to keep going I have left for today. She's probably just busy. Or maybe she's in an area with bad reception.

I fire up the browser and start searching the internet for Wallace Parcivall. There isn't much to be found. His obituary is the most comprehensive piece of information I can find, and the most important bits of it Ross already told me. Except he didn't mention that Wallace, known to friends and family as Wally, was widowed and is survived by two children, a son, and a daughter. Their names aren't listed.

The write up also includes a long-winded history of his military exploits. Apparently, he earned his stars by being the man for the job in several international crises. For a time in the 1990s, he even acted as an advisor to the US President. But I'll have to wait for his file to get the full details on all of that since it's clearly not public knowledge.

I close the browser and start typing up the request, keeping it brief and to the point. I plan on handing it to Thompson personally in the morning, while explaining the rest, which I'd rather not put into writing.

My phone buzzes as I'm waiting for the letter to print, and I'm so sure it's Eva—so happy it's her, more like—that my stomach clenches in disappointment when I see it's Ross again.

"The DNA lab discovered something, Sir," he tells me. "It's significant."

I tell him I'll be right there and hang up quickly before I say something meaner.

I can't help myself. This case is just one frustration after another and every time I start to hope the investigation has finally gotten wings, it grinds to a halt again, the sensation not unlike running headfirst into a brick wall. It was like that after the first two murders too, and I'm heartily sick of it.

Down at the lab, Ross and Wanda are waiting for me in the main room. Marisa's computer room is uncharacteristically dark, as is the office Blackman appropriated for his use. Maybe he's finally gone out to do some investigating in the field, and I'm kind of annoyed he didn't discuss that with me at all.

"What is it?" I ask since neither of them is volunteering the information.

Wanda blinks at me, her mouth open, but no sound coming out. Ross nudges her in a way he probably thinks I don't see.

"Right, Sir," she says. "We have a DNA match, well not really a match, a strange connection, a half match."

Her shyness makes her ramble, and I know that. I feel bad for getting annoyed and it takes a genuine effort not to snap at her to hurry up and get to the information.

She clears her throat, fixes her glasses, and looks at me again. "The hair that was found with the photographs is a familial match to the DNA found on the bodies."

Whoa. That information was almost worth waiting for. "Which DNA, the one from the rapes or the one found under one of the victim's fingernails?"

"From the rapes," she stammers.

"Familial as in what? Father and daughter?" I ask.

"They have half the alleles in common, which signifies a close familial match, meaning they are close relatives, but I can't tell you for certain whether that match is father-daughter, sister-brother or mother-son," she rattles off. The only time she's not timid and stuttering is when she's explaining science.

I wish she had more to give me, but this is already plenty.

I dismiss Ross and Wanda and retreat to the room Blackman's been using as his office. After a while of looking at the way he laid out the photos and the reports, I'm seeing no new connections and nothing to suggest that he found a solid one either.

Yet the curtains seem to be parting on the why of these murders, but what's behind them is still hazy and nondescript. Whatever the motive behind these killings is, it seems to have some kind of family component. Revenge for a wrongful death at the hands of a military man? Parcivall? Did he fake his own death and has now emerged as this Fairytale Killer? Or is he the original victim? Maybe his children blame the military for his death somehow and are using scenes from fairytales to let us know. But I don't see a woman's hand in these murders. They're too cold, too methodical, almost to the point of diabolical. And revenge is a hot emotion. Even when it's being served cold, it's never as icily detached as these murders appear.

All that is human was stripped from the victims in order to turn them into fictional characters. Even their blood. With all the serial killers I've studied, there was always a human element to it, something that connected the victim and the killer. But that's not the case with this killer. He doesn't even lay hands on them until after they're dead. Even his method of killing his victims is detached. He poisons them. And while poison is a woman's weapon, it is considered such because most women lack the physical strength to kill and dispose of a body. And everything about this case screams of physical strength. The bleeding, the posing, the carrying of a dead body up the stairs of the church tower, for pity's sake.

Unless it's two people working in tandem, dividing the roles according to their skills.

All of that is possible, but none of it is more possible than the next thing. Frustration-inducing at every turn. That's the only certainty in this case.

Eva still hasn't contacted me.

And I'm just about frustrated enough to go bang on her door and demand why. But that will lead to a massive argument that we might never recover from. I'm good at ending relationships, and completely inept at keeping them going, so I know that'd be a great way of ending this one. No. She just needs to cool off, and so do I.

I can't tell Schmitt what I've found, not yet, not if it leads to a two-star General, but I can go help interview some more of the junkies. Pretty soon they'll start needing their next fix badly enough to tell us everything we want to know, I'm sure of it.

23

EVA

I try to remember how I got here. But the icy cold spread from my neck all over my body in seconds. His vice-like grip on my forearm and his heavy arm around my neck was the only thing holding me up, as even my legs stopped working. He dragged me to a car parked on the sidewalk. A small van. White, I think. Parked between two large piles of snow already mostly black from the grime of the city.

The last thing I promised myself before even the fuzzy, round lights of the world faded to black, was that I'd remember the way, that I'd fight unconsciousness and know where he took me.

Instead, I woke up lying on a thin, bumpy mattress, its twisted and bent coils poking me in the back and legs. My head is resting on a hard, thin pillow, which is already making the back of my head and neck ache.

I've been here a while. The drug he injected me with is wearing off.

But my mind is far from clear, and I can't see.

My heart tries to race as I realize that, but it can't so it just sends sharp, painful cramps through my chest and into my left arm.

It's just a blindfold. My eyelashes scrape against the soft cloth of it as I open them, and I can see something, just not much, not anything I can recognize. The blindfold is thick, wide, and soft, its edges tickling the bridge of my nose.

I can't move either. My wrists and ankles are tied to the edges of the bed so firmly I can only move my legs and arms a few centimeters in either direction. The bindings are soft against my flesh, padded, the kind they use to restrain patients in hospitals.

In that tiny part of my mind the drug he gave me didn't muddle, I'm screaming, fighting against being restrained like this, like a piece of meat. My worst fear has always been being unable to move, being paralyzed. I can't even stand inside the four walls of my apartment, and it's a fairly large apartment, without needing to go out for at least an hour. How can I lay in bed and not move?

But the panic doesn't reach the muscles in my arms and legs. Doesn't even cut through the dense fog clouding the rest of my mind very deeply.

I have to concentrate. I have to clear the fog from my brain.

Smell and hearing are the only two senses left to me.

They're not telling me much.

A faint scent of snow, pristine and deep, hangs over the room. I can smell the mildew and damp of the mattress and old sweat on the pillow, sour and nasty. The room itself smells of wood and bleach. There's a muskiness underneath, something unclean, like this is a room in an old house that's impossible to clean thoroughly anymore. Another kind of scent grows thicker every so often, before fading away. It reminds me of raw meat.

I can hear wood creaking as though the house is settling around me for the evening. Or maybe it's footsteps. The silence in my prison is so thick it's like a blanket over my head. I can hear the wind rattling against the window, making it chime, the way the messed up window in my apartment chimes. When that happens, the smell of snow intensifies and a freezing cold draft wafts over my bare legs and arms.

If I could get free of my restraints, I could escape out that broken window.

If I focused enough on clearing my head. If he came back in and undid my restraints.

He called me Snow White.

The blond man Mirela described. Selima's boyfriend. The one who lured her to her death with his sweet voice and handsome face. The Fairytale Killer.

Why didn't I run?

Why didn't I recognize him?

Why didn't I fight?

I've taken several self-defense classes. I have a black belt in Judo. But I was dazzled by his charming smile, awed by his chiseled body, and hypnotized by the lustful desire in his eyes.

Mark will find me.

And hopefully, forgive me for being stupid enough to get snatched.

And hopefully, before I'm dead and cold and posed as my least favorite of all the princesses.

24

MARK

I was right about the junkies. By ten PM several of them were shaking as though they've spent the last day in the freezing cold and not the pleasantly warm cells and interview rooms of the police station. More of them were puking faster than the mess could be cleaned up.

Eventually, more and more started telling the same story, about a blond man who looked too healthy and too strong to be one of them hanging around, claiming to be one of them, hitting on the girls, never actually sleeping in the squat but always there in the evenings. He told everyone he worked security in one of the clubs in the area, but had lost his job recently and had nowhere to live, and by all accounts, no one doubted him, because he looked like a bouncer.

"He didn't belong, you know, man," the junkie I'm

interviewing says thorough chattering teeth. His face is covered with festering acne, and there's a nasty sore in the right corner of his mouth which I don't think will go away without medical intervention. A thick cloud of stench surrounds him—sour vomit, greasy hair, sweat, and the mix of various body odor varieties mixed into one single ball of unbearable stench. I had to fight not to gag each time I got a particularly rank whiff of it. Schmitt walks in, but the junkie barely notices. His eyes are focused on me, but something tells me he can't even see my face properly.

"He hit on this girl I was sort of seeing and then she was just gone one day, so I followed him one night, to see if he took her somewhere," he says. "I would've challenged him, but he was too big and too strong. He would've killed me. And the girl, I didn't know her that well and she wasn't all that far gone yet, she might have gone home or something, I didn't want to get beat up if she just went home, you know. Man, I need a hit."

He's been rambling like this for the past half an hour. They all were. But he's the only one who's offered more than a description of the guy, and the fight with the Russian thugs.

"You followed him?" I ask, patiently and friendly-like. Both my patience and friendliness are completely faked. "Where to?"

"This apartment, not far from the squat, a regular apartment, the kind you rent—"

"Where?" I ask before the rambling starts again.

"I don't know the address. She wasn't there. I stayed

looking up at the windows of the apartment and never saw her there, so I left. She never came back, but he did, a couple of days later. But like I said, she might've gone home," he says.

"Who was she?" I ask. "What was her name?"

"Lara," he says. "Maybe Lana. She wasn't from here, she was from Denmark."

I shoot Schmitt a look and he's already looking at me pointedly, probably thinking the same thing I'm thinking. The first Sleeping Beauty was Lara Dunholm, a beauty queen from Denmark.

"Can you show us where the apartment was?" Schmitt asks.

He nods, his eyes sparkling. At the prospect of getting out of here, no doubt.

"Good," I say and follow Schmitt out of the interview room.

"Can we bring him in if we find him?" I ask, since I'm not sure what we just heard is enough to detain someone under German law.

"I'll make it work," he says determinedly and tells me to wait close by. I go into the small kitchen and drink two glasses of water before pouring myself the last of the coffee. My headache's threatening to come back.

He has a group of uniformed officers and a prison transport van ready to go within a quarter of an hour.

So less than an hour later we're standing in front of a low apartment building on the northern edge of the Prenzlauer Berg district, not far from where the new buildings are going up. This one's seen better days. Graffiti so thick it's hard to decipher any one of them individually cover the grey facade, and the front door, once grand, tall and heavy, is hanging off the hinges and gaping open because of it.

"That one," the junkie says, pointing at the tall, dark window of a ground-floor apartment to the left of the door.

"We go in and knock?" Schmitt asks and I nod.

"What about me? Can I split?" the junkie asks. "I told you what you needed to know."

"Soon," I promise him. "We just need you to confirm that we got the right guy first."

After that, we'll probably have to let him go.

I don't envy the officer that will have to stay with him in the squad car, because he is rank.

Schmitt instructs his officers to make sure all the exits from the building are secured, then motions me and two uniformed officers to accompany him into the building.

The hallway is barely any warmer than outside and the fluorescent bulb which turns on automatically as we enter gives off more noise—a high pitched buzzing—than actual light.

The uniforms get into position, one on each side of the door, while I stand a step behind Schmitt at the door. He knocks loudly, the police knock designed to gain the upper hand before any of the action has even started and which is the same the world over.

"Police, open up!" he yells and takes half a step back from the door.

He has to knock and call two more times before the sound of locks being unlocked is finally followed by a bleary-eyed man wearing just boxers and a t-shirt opens the door.

"What is this?" he asks, the aggression in his voice dampened by early morning slurring.

"I'm Detective Schmitt of Criminal Investigations Unit, Homicide Division," Schmitt answers. "And you are wanted for questioning in relation to a missing person case."

"I thought you said you worked homicide," the man says mockingly.

Schmitt looks as tired as I feel, and he winces at the question. "We will have time enough to chat at the station. Put on some clothes and come with us."

He says it with enough power and authority that the man seems to be out of mocking questions. Schmitt and the officers wait at the door, but I need some fresh air. My headache is back, and it's getting worse.

And the night is just beginning. Even though it's almost morning, grey already pushing away the darkness to the east. I hope this isn't another false start. I don't know how many more of those I can take.

The junkie took one look at the man we brought out of the building and confirmed it's the man he knows from the squat. But that was as far as our luck held.

Schmitt and I have been taking turns interviewing the man for the past eight hours, taking turns with him in the stuffy, windowless interview room. It's so stuffy and close inside I'm seeing double if I move my head too fast. And my whole back, from the top of my head to my ass, is one giant pain that I can't even tell the origin of.

First, the guy lied about his name, saying it was James Hayes. Then he finally admitted he was Robert Greaves and after that, he refused to say much more. His DNA is on file from the rape charge he faced a few years ago, but the comparison to the DNA found on the bodies proved inconclusive. He refused to give another sample. As is apparently his right over here too.

At first, Schmitt balked at my suggestion to get his DNA from a soda bottle we offered him, saying he's not sure how legal that is. But he saw it my way once I explained that we just need to either eliminate or confirm him for now, and we'll worry about the actual evidence later. Maybe it's not the best way to handle this, but we're running out of options and leads. I'm afraid the longer we dally the more of a chance that a new body will turn up.

I'm on my way to the lab at the base with Greaves' soda bottle sealed in a large evidence bag. I'm so tired that the headlights of on-coming cars are blinding me worse than usual and leaving disturbingly bright, zigzagging flickers at the edges of my vision after they pass. Getting to the base without crashing will probably use up the last of my luck.

Marisa's behind her wall of computers and Blackman is in his office, his back turned to the empty main room. A map of Berlin and the surrounding area is taking up much of its interactive surface, red dots glowing in the spots where the bodies were found. Someone drew a blue line to connect them all, but if they form a pattern it's a very confusing one. Completely random, if you ask me.

I know better than to barge through the stainless steel doors to the area where the actual labs are, so I press the intercom, and tell the woman who answers what I need. Blackman is standing in the doorway of his office looking at me as I explain to the woman in a white jumpsuit complete with hood and goggles that comes to collect the evidence bag what I need done. And that I need it done fast.

"So you've taken my advice and are checking the rape kits from those other murders?" Blackman says, his tone flat.

I shake my head. "Those didn't match. This is Robert Greaves' DNA. The former soldier's accused of rape and discharged a couple of years ago." I walk over to him after the lab tech leaves.

"That's disappointing," he says as he steps back into his office. I follow. "I really thought we had something there."

"That's what this case is, one disappointment after another," I say, checking his desk. As far as I can tell everything is still laid out exactly as it was when I was here last. "Did you discover anything new?"

"Nothing. This case truly is frustrating in how every piece of evidence leads to a dead-end," he says, sinking into a chair with a sigh.

I don't follow suit. "I'm going to get a few hours of sleep while this DNA is processing. Maybe this will finally lead somewhere."

"Hope dies last. Isn't that what they say?" Blackman says, turning to me and grinning, a mocking gleam in his eyes. I don't appreciate it.

"Something like that, yes," I say and take my leave.

I am going home, but not before I visit Eva's apartment one more time. I've been calling her every couple of hours, each time promising it's the last time, and she still hasn't returned any of my calls. I even walked by her apartment building last night but didn't go in. All the windows were dark anyway, but they should be lit up now, as she wakes up and gets ready for her day. I might not be great at relationships, or even middling, but what we had was something great and I deserve more than being ignored. I deserve a straight answer and one way or another I will get it.

25

EVA

I think he gives me something to deaden my mind. Each time the fog in my mind starts to lift, he comes. He's soft-spoken and gentle, even his breath barely audible. He spoon-feeds me a thin overcooked vegetable broth. I spit the first spoonful out, aiming at his face, but I missed, hitting my bare arm instead.

He admonished me softly and gently as he wiped it away with a warm, moist cloth that smelled of lemons. Like those towels they give you on airplanes.

I demanded he untie me. I demanded to know why I was here. Where here was. I didn't expect answers, and I didn't get them. The darkness behind the blindfold and lying on my back, tied down to this smelly bed are starting to drive me crazy. But only for those few minutes when my mind is clear. After that the fog is everything. I hang somewhere between sleep and wakefulness, only that clear and alert part of my mind awake, buried deep beneath the fog and afraid. Terrified.

I spit out the second spoonful he tried to feed me too.

The softness and gentleness were gone then. He poured the soup down my throat, then pinched my nose together and held my mouth shut until I swallowed. Over and over he did this, until the fog started rolling in thick over my thoughts again. The drug must be in the soup.

The next time he came, I accepted the spoon and ate on my own.

I have no idea how long I've been kept here.

Days, weeks, months? Nothing makes any sense. Except for the knowledge that I'm to be his next dead princess. That's always the first thought that lights up when the fog in my brain parts.

26

MARK

The windows of Eva's place were dark, but I went up anyway, banged on the door, and called her name until several neighbors came to see what was going on. Including a little girl still in her nightgown, clutching a stuffed rabbit, long wavy blonde hair falling around her face, and nearly covering it. She followed her father into the hall.

He's the one that told me he's calling the police if I don't leave right away, and I almost told him to go right ahead and do that, but the sad, scared little eyes looking up at me from behind his back silenced me better than his angry threats.

I went to my apartment after that and fell asleep in my clothes and shoes, and on top of the covers, no less.

My headache and backache are only slightly better when my landline phone wakes me with its modern, robotic imitation of the classic ringtone. It takes me a while to know where the ringing is coming from since I don't think I ever got a call on the landline since moving in here.

"Hold for Major-General Thompson," a woman's voice says once I finally pick up the phone and grumble a hello into it.

"You're a hard man to get a hold of this morning, Major," Thompson says. I check my watch. It's nearly noon.

"I came home for a couple of hours to sleep," I say.

"Only right," he says. "That file you requested, it will be here in two days."

"I completely forgot to put in the request for it," I mutter, not realizing I spoke aloud until hearing my own voice.

"That was just a formality," Thompson says. "I was able to request the file, but it wasn't easy. General Parcivall was an important man, with many friends in high places. A few of them have already called me, demanding to know why I'm requesting his file."

"His print was found on one of the photos the Germans received. The Snow White photo, if I'm not mistaken."

"Yes, Major, I know that. But I didn't mention it to any of the callers," Thompson says. "You can check the file when it arrives, but it's for your eyes only, is that clear?"

"Yes, Sir," I say automatically.

"And we won't be mentioning the Parcivall name in

connection with this investigation until it's clear that there is a connection. Mention it to no one, not even Colonel Blackman. I've already spoken to Sargent Ross and gave him the same instructions. Is that understood as well?"

"Yes, Sir," I say again, completely alert now. Something in Thompson's voice tells me it was hard getting the file, that those calls he received weren't just inquisitive in nature.

"You understand I have to be adamant about this, given how you handled this investigation in the past," Thompson says, a little less harshly.

"This time the connection is clear cut and obvious, Sir," I say. If not logical in the least. But I don't add that.

"Keep me posted," he says and hangs up.

I sit on the edge of the bed and rub my eyes, which feel like hot sand's been poured into them while I slept. I dare not stretch, afraid that'll make the kinks in my neck and back worse.

Shower first, I decide, hoping cold water will wake me up.

It does, somewhat, and my eyes are more or less back to normal too, as I finally check my phone. I have twenty unanswered calls, most from the base, three from Schmitt, none from Eva.

I check the thirty texts before returning any of the calls.

One of those is from Eva. From her work phone, the one she never calls or texts me from unless it's an emergency and her personal phone is out of battery.

My hands are shaking and my chest is compressed like a heavy rock is resting on it.

Find me.

I read it five times before I finally accept that's all she wrote.

It's not like her to play games. And she'd always sooner say too much than too little, even if it gets her in trouble.

The rock pressing against my chest is as heavy as an elephant as I dial the number she texted me from. The annoying robotic lady that answers tells me my call cannot be completed at this time, first saying it in German then repeating it in English. The standard message when a phone is off or out of range. I call her personal phone next and this one rings. Hope welling up in my chest as the third ring is interrupted by someone picking up is so strong it nearly chokes me.

"Hello?" a timid female voice answers, dashing that hope right in the bud.

"This is Major Mark Novak, I would like to speak to Eva," I say in a split second decision I'd better handle this professionally and not like a maniacal jilted lover.

"She's...umm...is that the woman whose phone this is?" the timid voice asks.

"Who is this?" I ask. "Why are you answering this phone?"

"I'm Gitta. I work at Buch Cafe Haus on Karl-Marx-Allee," she says. "A blonde lady lost this phone outside a couple of days ago. We thought she'd come back for it since she's a regular, but she hasn't and it's been ringing and ringing. So I picked up."

I didn't know fear this strong could be felt. It's in my veins, carried everywhere by my blood.

"I'll be right there," I say. "Please don't go anywhere until I get there."

I tell myself over and over that everything's fine, that this is all just a misunderstanding, that she just lost her phone and doesn't know it yet. Somehow, it lets me get dressed, instead of just running there half-dressed and with no shoes on.

But it's not fine. Eva never goes anywhere without that phone.

27

EVA

I'm untied!

Or one of my arms is.

A warm, coarse hand is massaging my right wrist, the fingers long and bony. Not the same man who grabbed me in the street. That man had huge, strong hands with stubby fingers that held my arm hard enough to bruise.

He's humming softly, under his breath. It sounds like a lullaby.

This is my chance!

I pull my arm out of his grasp. I'll kick him, incapacitate him and escape out the window.

All I manage is a jerk.

My body won't obey my mind's command.

"Settle down now, lovely girl," he says in that same singsong voice he was using before. "It will all be over soon. It will all be well soon."

He reattaches the restraint to my wrist, hope fleeing my chest like air from a popped balloon.

"You sick, twisted, bastard!" I yell, but it comes out like a cracked, hoarse whisper.

He laughs. It's a pleasant laugh, warm and kind and it sours my stomach to the point of nausea. I smell no soap on him today. Only old man breath and shaving cream. As I recognize the scent, I also feel the tightness in the skin of my legs and arms. The foul monster shaved me while I slept. Shaved me everywhere.

"Such a foul mouth on such a lovely princess," he says. "But we'll cure that soon enough."

"You don't have to do this," I say, deciding to change tactics. When kidnapped, it's best to try and make your captor see you as a human being. Then they might let you go. Though I doubt there is anything human left in this monster, despite his soft voice, gentle touch, and pleasant laugh. "I have a life, a good life. I never saw your face, you can just let me go."

He runs his hand through my hair. "Such a lovely shade of hair you have. It's almost a shame to ruin it," he says as though I haven't spoken. "But blue-black will look striking with those big, bright blue eyes of yours. We'll dye it as soon as my son returns."

My breath hitches. There's two of them working together? Mark is only looking for one. The son, I presume. The one who grabbed me, the one Selima dated. I have to tell him.

I whimper, tears welling in my eyes, getting soaked up by my thick blindfold, as reality hits me.

I'll never tell Mark anything ever again. Not even that I love him.

28

MARK

I run/walk to the coffee shop instead of taking the car, because the narrow streets around there are always jammed up with traffic, even at midday. The people I pass are a blur of white and black and red when they yell and curse at me for bumping into them. My mind is so laser-focused on getting to the coffee shop, getting to Eva, that I feel nothing and care less about anyone or anything.

It's her favorite coffee shop in the city. I met her there at least ten times since we started dating. We had one of our best dates in there, did things in one of the more private upstairs rooms that I haven't even thought of doing since I was in my early twenties, things that made me feel young. I believed she was the one who'd make me feel forever young, even at eighty. Now what? Now I'm already thinking of her in the past tense. How could I believe she'd willingly not answer my calls or come to the door when I knocked? How much time did I waste?

I'm breathing hard as I burst into the coffee shop, the heat inside making my already overheated face unbearably hot.

"Are you Gitta?" The young woman behind the counter, her thick brown hair reaching down to her ass has every reason to look alarmed. She nods slowly, her brown eyes huge in her round face.

I take a couple of deep breaths and introduce myself more calmly and tell her why I'm here.

She reaches under the counter without taking her scared eyes off me and hands me Eva's phone. There's a single crack running diagonally along the screen, starting from a tiny shattering in one corner where the metal around the screen is also bent. She dropped her phone. My heart clenches at the memory of how flustered she was each time that happened to her—not often, because she was careful with her electronics—and how childishly happy she was to find it whole. I used to tell her she was too attached to her gadgets when that happened and I'm very, very sorry for that now. And here I go thinking about her like she's gone again.

"Where did you find this phone?" I ask, focusing on the woman in front of me and asking the right questions. If I let myself get lost in fear and panic, I'll never find Eva. "And when?"

I have a sinking feeling I know exactly when. The

night I stood her up at the last minute.

"Dieter, can you come here," the woman calls over her shoulder and a tall, very skinny boy with a spray of dark red pimples on both cheeks turns to her. "This man is asking about the phone you found."

Dieter approaches warily, glancing at the phone and then me several times before reaching the counter.

"Where did you find this phone? And when?" I repeat the questions to get him to focus on me.

He looks up and to the left like he's trying to remember. "It was two nights ago, I think. Yes, two nights. I was outside, having a cigarette when she walked out. The blonde lady, Eva, she's a regular and the only one who orders chamomile tea."

"And where did she go? Which direction?" I ask before he starts telling me about all the other things she liked to order here.

"She met this guy outside. He looked like he was jogging, though he was dressed very lightly for it. Just shorts and a sleeveless shirt. But these boot camp workout fanatics are crazy enough for that, so I didn't think too much of it. They talked and then he put his arm around her and led her off. It was only afterward that I noticed she dropped her phone. It glinted as a car passed on the street. I called after her, but she didn't hear me. I even ran after her, but they were already in a car and driving away."

My heart feels still in my chest. If I think about anything other than the questions I must ask this kid, I'll lose my mind and never find it again.

"What kind of car?" I ask.

"A white minivan, like the kind they take people on tours with," he says. "Maybe a Volkswagen. Or a Mercedes."

"Did you get the license plate?" I ask.

He shakes his head. "Sorry, no. But it was local. I saw that much. And I couldn't see inside the van, because all the shades on the windows were closed."

"And the man, what did he look like?"

"Muscular, his arms were wider than both my legs. He was at least a head taller than her, and broad across the shoulders. Blond. Looked very happy to see her. Like a kid happy."

Whatever that means.

"He reminded me of Jack Nicholson playing Joker," the kid says to Gitta, who gives him a half-smile, then focuses her attention back on me. "His smile did, that is, the way it twisted up at the edges so unnaturally. I couldn't figure it out until just now."

Crazy, in other words. Unhinged.

"Did he have any tattoos?"

The young man nods eagerly. "Lots and lots. On his legs and his arms. Even had those stupid eagle wings or whatever they are on the back of his neck. Those are so ridiculous."

Greaves has no wings on his neck. I pull out my phone and show the kid a photo of Greaves anyway, turning it so Gitta, who's following our conversation with such rapture her mouth is half-open, can't see it. "Was this him?"

The kid peers at the photo for a full minute before shrugging. "Maybe. It's possible."

I scroll to the photo of the sketch Mirela provided. "What about this one?"

He looks at the photo then back at me. "That's the same guy, isn't it?"

Maybe. I don't know. There are so many tall blond guys with near-perfect features around here.

"He looked more like the sketch than the photo, I'd say," the man says. "But they both look very alike. Who is this guy, anyway? Is he dangerous? Or is he just the guy she left you for? I remember you coming in here with her."

He's being arrogant like all men his age are. Like I was. So I let it slide.

"He's wanted by the police," I tell him instead. "Can you come with me to the station to answer some more questions?"

"What now?" he asks. "My shift doesn't end until two."

"Yes, now. This is important."

"So's my job man," he says. "I'll be there at two. Or half-past."

"Go, I'll cover for you," Gitta says to him and I thank her silently, but from the bottom of my heart. "It sounds urgent."

The kid agrees but takes his sweet time getting his jacket and bag from the back. I call Schmitt and explain I'll be bringing in a witness as I lead him through the crowded street to the station.

It's only been two days. There's still a chance we'll find her. We have a description of a car and a description of the man who took her. I can still find her. I can still save her. I can.

I'm setting such a pace through the crowded streets my witness is having a hard time keeping up despite his long legs. I have to keep stopping to wait for him, which annoys me so much I want to yell at him each time, but somehow I'm managing not to. Maybe it's because the time I spent with Eva is playing in my mind in a series of perfectly vivid, colorful scenes, distracting me from everything else. Is this what they mean when they talk about your life flashing before your eyes?

We finally reach the avenue that leads to the police HQ building. Three gleaming black cars with tinted windows so dark they're as black as the cars themselves are parked about two-hundred meters from the main entrance. The witness is breathing hard behind me as we approach the cars, whispering under his breath. Cursing most likely.

The back door of the front-most car opens just as I'm about to pass it and the Russian mobster Alexeyev steps out to block my path, waving at someone in one of the other cars before fixing his black eyes on me.

"Hello, Inspector Novak," he says. "I've been trying to reach you."

"I'm in a hurry," I tell him and keep walking. The last thing I need is this distraction right now. Only one thing matters right now. Finding Eva before she's turned into a dead princess. With how badly the search for this Fairytale Killer has gone so far, I probably don't stand a chance in hell, but I refuse to think about that.

"You have time for this," Alexeyev says in a very self-assured voice. He's not giving an order, he's just stating a fact.

Two large, beefy guys wearing identical baggy, black leather jackets that were very popular at the end of the last century are approaching me, supporting an equally beefy guy between them. The guy's only wearing jeans and no shoes or shirt. Tattoo of every kind cover his torso and arms, but they're all covered with dried blood. His hair is most likely blond, but it's red from all the blood he's lost. His face is in better shape than I would've expected given all the blood, and he looks at me with bright blue eyes so full of insanity, it takes every ounce of self-control I possess not to step back from him.

"I told you I will find him for you," Alexeyev says. "This is the man who took my Nadia. My guys confirmed it already."

The guy keeps staring at me like we're the only two people in the street. His lips are curled up at the edges, making him look even more maniacal. He can't stand on his own. The Russian thugs holding one of his arms each had to drag him to get him this far.

"That's the man I saw with Eva," my witness says. "See how he smiles. Just like Joker."

"Thank you," I say to Alexeyev. What else do you say to a guy who just made the impossible possible?

"Get this bastard," he says. "I would've done it myself, but then I thought maybe he has other girls like my Nadia locked up somewhere. He won't talk. No matter what we did to him, he just smiled."

And they did a lot. Clearly they tried very hard to harm him. The fingers on his right hand are hanging off his hand crookedly, uselessly, while three on his left are missing, the stumps burned closed by the looks of things. There are also several burn scars on his chest and neck, the kind caused by high voltage electrical shocks.

"I'll take it from here," I say and wave over the uniformed police officers who are already watching us.

The thugs let the man drop to the pavement and hurry to the car. Alexeyev gets back into his as well, and they're all speeding away before the officers even reach us.

"Get Schmitt," I tell the first one that reaches us, and grab the witness' arm to push him forward. "And take this kid to him. He's a witness."

"What about this guy," another officer asks, kneeling beside the man on the ground. He can't get up on his own, but he's twisting his head so he can keep grinning at me. It's making me sick.

"Get him to an interview room," I say.

"He needs to go to the hospital," the officer protests.

"He needs to go to an interview room," I say. "This is the man we've been looking for. Bring a doctor to him there."

All the officers that heard me speak paled, each understanding what I meant even though I didn't call him by his nickname. The Fairytale Killer. Well, this guy won't be sewing any pretty princess outfits anymore, not without his fingers. But if losing half his left hand didn't make him talk, how am I gonna do it?

So close and yet so far. That sums up this entire case perfectly. From start to finish. But it's not over yet. And I won't give up until it is.

I rush after the officers taking the suspect into the building. A crowd of people has gathered to watch us, most of their faces twisted in fear and disgust as the two officers half carry and half drag the bloodied man inside. I'm sure they wouldn't be as disgusted at this treatment if they knew who he is. It's the same inside the reception area, which is very full for this time of day, and where people are actually standing up on the wooden benches to get a better look. Some are taking pictures. One camera flash goes off directly in my eyes, leaving me with a huge lava red spot lined with fire in my vision. I wish they weren't taking pictures. I wish I knew how to stop them before those pictures make it online.

Schmitt is waiting for us by the elevators on the

third floor.

"What's going on? What is this?" he says, uncharacteristic nervousness in his voice.

"I'll explain later," I say. "He needs to be questioned."

He makes a similarly disgusted face as he looks at the suspect as the people downstairs were making. "He needs a doctor."

"This might be him," I say pointedly and watch Schmitt's face freeze, all color leaving it.

"Interview Room 5," he tells his officers.

That's one of the smaller rooms, but the one closest to the elevators. The way there is a blur of color and snippets of conversation that don't form a comprehensive whole in my head.

The suspect's grin looks forced once I'm facing him across the cheap, chipped artificial wood veneer-topped table in the interrogation room. The metal legs of my chair wobble as I sit down, but I already feel like I'm falling anyway, so it makes no difference.

"You won't find her in time," the man says in English, speaking for the first time. Good English, the kind spoken by rich people on the East Coast.

One of his bright blue eyes looks glassy. I'm not sure he can see me with it. But the other is still filled with that maniacal light of pure insanity.

"Tell me where Eva is," I say, just asking for what I need and nothing else.

"By now she's not Eva anymore. She's Snow White," he says.

I leap out of my chair, sending it bouncing off the

THE FAIRYTALE KILLER

floor. "You sick, deranged, twisted—"

"Call me all the names in the book, if you want. It won't save her," he says slowly, measuredly. No pain is showing on his face, even though he must be in considerable pain from his injuries. I don't know if that's because he's insane or because his brain isn't working properly anymore. Why the fuck did the Russians have to torture him? But I know why. Revenge. And I want some too.

"My father won't wait much longer for me," he says. "He'll create the scene with your lovely reporter girlfriend without me if he must. She cries, you know. She hopes you'll save her. But you won't, will you?"

Strong arms pull me back as I leap at him. "No!" Schmitt says curtly through gritted teeth. He's stronger than he looks, his arms are like steel ropes holding me back. He's panting as he pulls me out of the room. I'm resisting, but he's managing it. The suspect starts laughing. A quiet, eerie laugh. It sounds like it's coming from very far away.

Outside, Schmitt pushes me against the wall and holds me there with one wiry forearm across the chest. "That man's been hurt bad. He needs to go to the hospital or he will die on us."

Good. Just as long as he tells me where Eva is first.

"Calm down," Schmitt adds, his black eyes piercing. "He has your girlfriend and I understand how much you want to get her back. But losing our minds with him is not going to help us any. You know this, Mark. You said it to me often enough."

Slowly, his words are starting to make sense.

I try to wriggle out of his hold, but he's not releasing me. "All right, I'm calm. Let me go. I won't go back in."

He gazes into my eyes for a few seconds as though to see if I'm telling the truth. Eventually, he lets me go.

"Come into my office," he says, and I follow him down the hall. We have to weave our way between much too closely placed desks in the open area in front of his small office. Junior detectives get desks in the open area, but Schmitt has his own tiny office. The wall facing the open room is part window, part drywall, and Schmitt hastily lowers the blinds over the former as soon as the dark wood door is closed behind us.

Inside, every available surface, including his desk, both chairs, and part of the floor is covered with photos, reports, documents, maps, and handwritten notes. I trample some of them under my feet as I walk to the chair and sweep a bunch more off before sitting down. I need to sit. That surge of adrenaline where I almost beat up our only suspect is not fading easily. It's making me see double while the room spins around me.

"What's happening?" Schmitt asks. "Explain it to me."

I do so in as few words as I can, recounting everything that I found out this morning, and how it led to the bloodied man in Interview Room 5. An invisible clock is ticking very loudly in my head as I do.

"There are cameras on many of the buildings along

the street where he grabbed her," I say. "I checked as we walked. They're on every intersection, or near enough. The recordings need to be accessed and searched. We're looking for a white minivan with curtained windows."

Schmitt is nodding.

"And Eva's phone, it has to be tracked," I say. "He sent me a text from it. Maybe he's getting careless and sent it from wherever he's holding her."

"I doubt that," Schmitt says, but snaps his mouth shut as I glare at him.

"And we need to move fast, you heard him, he's not working alone," I say. "His father is…"

What was I gonna say? Bleeding Eva as we speak? Gluing her wrists shut? Dressing her as Snow White? Raping her dead body?

I sway forward in my chair and almost throw up. I'm too late. Whatever I do now, it'll already be too late. This is just another dead end. But the crash at the end of it will be the worst yet. It'll be deadly.

"Are you well?" Schmitt asks, his voice betraying that he's sure I'm not.

I straighten up, take a few deep breaths and stand up. "I'm all right. Let's get to work."

He nods. "We'll start by checking the video footage and determine where he drove her to. We'll go right now, on foot, you and me, we'll view the videos as we go, and hopefully, we'll find the place he took her to in time."

He's still over-talking to me, and doing so very

calmly, which is a tactic I often use with distressed witnesses, victims, or relatives of the victims. It's embarrassing to have it used on me, but it's working. If I concentrate on his words and the plans he's making, I can kinda-sorta see beyond the insurmountable wall of panic that's crushed my ability to think straight and reason.

"Maybe we're not too late," Schmitt says. "If his father doesn't know we arrested him, he might still be waiting for him."

"All those people in reception taking photos," I say, my heart racing again as I slam open the door. "They'll be posting the photos all over social media."

This time Schmitt doesn't try to halt my mad dash across the open area, he's barking orders to lock down the building, and he's right behind me as I emerge into the hallway.

The four paramedics crowded around a gurney with our now-unconscious suspect, and the five officers surrounding them as they wait for the elevator, are taking up most of the space. I turn to the stairs, just as the elevator pings and the doors hiss open.

"No, don't stop me!" an angry voice says. "I will be heard!"

Then a dwarf, barely taller than my waist, elbows his way through the crowd in front of the elevator. I'm no longer sure whether I'm hallucinating, dreaming, or I've lost my mind in the sick, twisted fairytale this psycho is weaving for me. But the dwarf does look very familiar.

29

MARK

The dwarf is looking up at me, his hooded dark brown eyes angry enough to make me think they'll start shooting fire. He's wearing some type of costume under his light blue-grey parka—coarse, brown homespun pants cinched at the ankles, a white cotton shirt, and a doublet embroidered with vines and leaves. There are two identical red spots on his cheekbones, and the red pouf of his hat is hanging out his jacket pocket.

"You're investigating this serial killer, aren't you?" he asks me. "This Fairytale Killer?"

He's not much bigger than a ten-year-old, and I have to resist the urge to crouch down so we're at eye level.

"Yes," I say simply.

"I've been trying to talk to you for days," he says.

"My friends, well my colleagues were here a week ago for a special show we put on each year. They disappeared on the way to the airport. No one's seen them since. Their families are frantic with worry, calling me all the time, but they can't get anyone at the police station to take them seriously. There were seven of them. Seven dwarfs are missing."

He puts a lot of emphasis on those last two phrases, but I figured it out before he got to that part. I think I knew it the first time I saw him, I just didn't want to believe it.

Schmitt and I exchange a meaningful look. It's not a surprise no one was available to talk to this dwarf. It's been all hands on deck for catching The Fairytale Killer and a lot of things were going undone since the first of these last four bodies had turned up.

"He stages scenes for fairytales, doesn't he?" the dwarf asks, some of the fire gone from his voice. His eyes are unsure, but defiant too, like he's afraid we're going to start laughing at him. I've never been less inclined to laugh at anything in my life. "He needs seven dwarfs for Snow White."

"Come with us," Schmitt says, laying a hand on the dwarf's shoulder. "We'll talk somewhere more private."

He leads him into the first room that's open and empty and shuts the door firmly.

"I'm Detective Schmitt and this is Major Novak of the US Army," he says. "And yes, we are trying to catch the serial killer known as The Fairytale Killer. I am sorry you weren't listened to. We have been very busy."

"Please tell us everything you know," I say. "And as quickly as you can."

The dwarf sits in the chair Schmitt pulled out for him, then shrugs off his jacket, baring his shoulders. "So, this troop of dwarfs, they're from Ontario, Canada, and they were here at my invitation. Their flight back was last Friday evening."

"How were they traveling to the airport?" Schmitt asks, interrupting him. "Taxi? The train?"

"I was going to order them a ride from one of those private shuttle services that specialize in airport transports. We were talking about it in the lobby of their hotel and a man overheard us. Said he offered such services and that he could pick them up. Quoted a great rate, and they accepted."

"Was it the man the paramedics were working on out in the hall just now?" I ask.

"What man?" the dwarf asks.

I pull out the composite sketch.

He looks at it. "It might've been, I don't know. He had a baseball cap on, pulled low over his eyes. He was big and broad though. Kind of scary looking. But he spoke perfect English and I think that set them at ease. He even joked with them for a while, saying he knew of a couple of party spots he could take them to before their flight, to tire them out for the long journey. More than a few were ready to take him up on the offer. But I don't know if they did. I said my goodbyes and didn't hear from them again until their families started contacting me a couple of days later."

Schmitt is already holding his phone in his hand, ready to start issuing orders. "Which hotel was it?"

"The Alexanderplatz Holiday Inn," the dwarf says.

Schmitt thanks the dwarf, then tells him someone is going to come and take his statement again.

"Do you think they're still alive?" the dwarf asks.

Both Schmitt and I look at him, neither of us answering. I'm hoping Schmitt will say something soothing, and he's probably hoping I will.

"It's our hope we'll find them in time," Schmitt finally says, and he's speaking about Eva too, I know it, just as I know I wouldn't be able to speak without unraveling again. I can't unravel. I need to do what I can to find Eva while there's still hope. I can unravel once that's gone.

Most of the cameras filming the street where Eva was taken either didn't work, didn't record, or were so grainy not much was visible. We did find one that clearly showed the man—our suspect-lifting her in the front seat of a white minivan. But the image was so grainy, reading a license plate off it was a pipe dream. The best image enhancement program wouldn't have helped with that.

Our next stop was the Holiday Inn where a young, black-haired manager gave us nearly fifteen minutes of grief about needing court orders and warrants and whatnot before she could show us the security camera footage. She wore too much cloyingly sweet perfume and was so done up, her makeup, hair, and clothes all perfect, I'm sure she spends all the hours when she's not at work making herself look good. Eventually, she relented and let us view the footage.

And it was pure gold.

The indoor shots were grainy, but I could clearly see the suspect talking to a group of dwarfs, none taller than his waist. This was the event the dwarf at the police station described.

The next day, just before noon, the group of dwarfs checked out. Then, at noon precisely, they filed through the lobby, carrying their suitcases, and disappeared through the revolving doors onto the street.

The cameras outside are of much better quality than the ones in the lobby. The white minivan was clearly visible as it waited for them at the curb. As was the man, our suspect, helping them put their suitcases in the bag. The vehicle tag was clear too. Or at least a part of it. Local.

It was more than I hoped for. But I'm not sure it's enough.

We've been in the circular main room of the ultra-modern computer crime lab, which is located just a few blocks from the police HQ building. A huge screen, at least four by four meters in size dominates one side of the room. The desks with computers are all facing it and there have to be at least several workstations in there. Leave it to the Germans to do everything to the highest standard of utmost efficiency. Which includes their traffic camera system.

They were able to pick up the white minivan leaving the Holiday Inn and trace it all the way out of the city heading north. But he didn't get on the autobahn. He headed down a regional road, with no cameras.

I almost lost all hope right then, until one of the techs came up with the bright idea to check the service station cameras along that road, if there were any. There was one. The minivan passed it at just before two PM. By then it was in a rural area where there is only a few houses, not even proper villages and a couple of farms. Still too many places to search.

But we're going to search them.

I had them check the footage from the service station on the night Eva was taken too. One of them showed a white minivan passing at around eight PM. There was no way to read the tags on it, but I'm sure it's the same car.

I step away from the screen for some privacy and call Blackman. He's proven his worth deducing things right from just looking at maps, and I'm as close to praying he can do it again as I've ever been. The phone in the room he's using as his office rings and rings until I'm sure he's not going to pick up. But he does.

"We have a very promising lead on the place where the killer might be holding his victims," I tell him. "But it's still an area of about twenty square kilometers and we need to narrow it down."

"That's a huge area," he says. "Where is it?"

"A rural area about an hour to the north of Berlin city limits," I tell him. "Not that many houses, but a few large farmsteads. I want to narrow it down as much as I can before we go out there and start knocking on doors."

"Yes, that's a good idea," he says. "Where is it?"

I tell him everything I know, then ask him to get Marisa on board to help him set up the topographical satellite map of the area. She can't access all the information from there, but she's a resourceful young woman and a computer whiz. She'll do all she can.

When I return to the large screen, it's already showing the map, with bright white spots indicating houses.

"How do we narrow this down?" Schmitt asks. A tech is standing next to him, a short man with a shaved head, wearing round John Lennon-type glasses.

He was talking to him, I think, but I answer, "First we eliminate all the houses and farms that are occupied and have been occupied for the past five years."

I doubt this killer started operating that long ago, but we might need to widen that bracket if I'm wrong.

The tech is nodding, jotting it down.

"Then we eliminate any areas where the houses are clustered together," I continue. "This guy doesn't want witnesses."

"And then what?" the tech asks.

"If we're lucky, this will leave us with only a few places to search," I say. "You do have access to the kind of databases you need to check this stuff in, don't you?"

The tech looks at me like I'm soft in the head. "Yes, we have access to every database."

"Good, get to it please," Schmitt tells him.

There were ten people on duty when we came in, but more have been called in and there are now thirty of them looking up the information we need.

I wait by the screen, my arms folded over my chest, studying the satellite map and watching as clusters of houses get crossed out by big, red digital crosses as the techs eliminate them. I hate this part. I hate this waiting.

I want to be out there, going door to door, looking for Eva, not standing here at a map of where she might not even be. But this is my last shot at finding her alive. There won't be any more chances after this one. I know it in my bones and I can't even move, because that might cause a cascade of other movements that'll lead to me going out there and lumbering around, asking for her in all the wrong places, alerting the psycho in the process. I cannot screw this up.

Two hours later, the map shows only four possible places where The Fairytale Killer's lair could be. The techs could find detailed photos of only three of them. Abandoned farms all, uninhabited for a decade or more, each sprawled over several hectares of land with many buildings to search.

"I say we visit them all at the same time," Schmitt suggests.

"We'll be seen coming from far away," I say.

The big screen is now sectioned off into four squares, each showing one of the locations. Three are showing pictures of the farm buildings overlaid over the map, while the fourth just shows the map, an old photo of a huge orchard, and a long winding road snaking from the main road to the white dots that are the buildings of the farm. We have no idea what those are since the techs could find no recent pictures of it. The three we do have pictures of are all huge, multi-structure complexes. Two of them have smaller houses too, which could've been places for housing seasonal workers, or maybe the houses where other family members or permanent workers lived. I don't know much about farm life, but given how far from any town these places are, I'm guessing most of the staff lived on-site. And given the size of the land, staff size must've been considerable. Two of the places were chicken farms, one was a cattle farm, and the last, the one with no recent pictures, specialized in apple production before it failed some thirty years ago. That's the smallest of the lot, comprised of only three buildings and the one farthest away from the main road. That's the one I've picked to visit first.

My phone buzzes in my pocket, and I excuse myself

to go take the call. It's the base and I'm hoping they've found something I have not.

"Major Novak," Blackman says. "I have here the file of General Wallace Parcivall. Why have you requested this?"

He's speaking in a terse monotone voice, but I feel a seething of great anger underneath it. He wasn't supposed to know about the file. It was cleared for my eyes only.

"A connection to our case came up, and I decided to follow it up," I say. "It could be nothing."

"And it could be everything," Blackman says. "I investigated Parcivall more than fifteen years ago, in connection to the allegations that he was mistreating his children. I found he was torturing them. I also found compelling evidence that he murdered his wife. The man should've been locked up. Instead, the Army covered it all up. Returned the children to him and pretended all I found out was conjecture. That is the reason I resigned. It is the reason I refused to come on board for this case when Major-General Thompson first asked me six months ago."

I can hear the years of living with this frustration, of having to bottle it all up and watch the man he knew to be guilty as sin parade around as a free man.

"His daughter lost her mind in her teens and had to be institutionalized because of the abuse," Blackman says. "His son ran away and hid. He lived a very hard life on the streets for years. A life of crime. Their father was extolled a hero of the nation. Praised, esteemed, and highly decorated. It made me sick, but there was nothing I could do to prevent it. I tried everything. Those poor children. They only had me to speak for them and I failed them."

He's speaking like he's explaining it to me, looking for my forgiveness. In my twelve years as a CID Special Investigator, I've never had a case where the man or woman I found to be guilty of a crime went unpunished in the higher interest of the US Military, as was clearly the case here. If that had happened to me, I'd probably sound just as devastated and slightly mad with grief and the injustice of it all as he sounds right now.

"Do you think the children could be behind these killings?" I ask.

"The daughter, Rebecca, poor thing, killed herself almost two years ago. Her psychiatrists at the home she was in thought she was getting better and gave her more freedom. She cut her wrists with a razor she bought on her first unsupervised outing. Her body was found by a creek, two days after she left the institution for an hour in town."

She cut her wrists and bled out. The pieces of this puzzle are starting to fit.

"We have the son," I tell him. "He's at the hospital now, badly hurt, because the father of one of the dead women got to him first. The only thing he told us was that his father will carry out the killing without him."

Blackman gasps and doesn't exhale.

"Do you think his father could still be alive? Do you think they're in this together?"

Blackman doesn't say anything for a couple of moments and it takes all the self-control I have not to demand he answer.

He finally exhales and I hear crackling on the line like he's running his fingers through his hair.

"I doubt it. Russell hated his father. He ran away as soon as he could and stayed away as far as I know," he finally says.

"So, what? Did he take up with a man he now considers his father? A man crazy enough to help him commit these murders?"

"I doubt that," Blackman says slowly. "Russell was a lone wolf sort of child. Only really cared about his little sister. I doubt he'd partner up with anyone. He could just be riling you up. Telling you lies."

That's not what it sounded like when he said it. It sounded like gloating. Like he was rejoicing in the fact that I failed. He used the last of his strength to tell me that. But I don't explain all that to Blackman. We've wasted enough time on this trip down memory lane already.

"Did you look at the map?" I ask. "Do you have any idea where he might've been heading the night he abducted the dwarfs?"

And my girlfriend. But I don't say that. I wouldn't be able to get it off my tongue, I'd choke on the words.

"The easternmost one is closest to the road, but hidden behind tall pine trees and is a former cattle farm," he says. "I'd bet on that one since there's bound to be a slaughterhouse attached to it, complete with hooks and tools for bloodletting."

The image his words painted twist my stomach so painfully hard I gasp. Eva hanging from a hook by her perfect little feet, her blood slowly trickling from her body. And now I can't unsee it.

"I'm sorry," he blurts out and I don't want to hear anymore.

"That one's the biggest to search," I say. "It'll most likely take everyone the German's have at their disposal to send."

The farm is made up of ten buildings, most of them huge. It's spread out around a sizable courtyard complete with cow pens and pig pens and whatnot. He could be holding Eva in any one of those buildings. And as Blackman said, the trees would most likely allow him to see us before we see him.

"The other ones, especially the one with no good photos, are too remote," Blackman continues matter-of-factly. "He has to transport the bodies and the props and he wants it all to look perfect when it arrives at its destination. That to me says he'll want to drive over as little rough terrain as he can."

The one I have my eye on is twenty kilometers west of the one Blackman is suggesting. There's no telling what kind of condition the road leading up to it is, but it's probably safe to assume it has not been taken care of in the years since the farm has been out of commission. If Blackman's reasoning is sound, which it most likely is, then that is the last one the killer will pick as his hideout. But it's in the middle of nowhere and there's no village or town near it. If we approach through the fields where the apple trees once grew we might be able to surround its three buildings before he knows we're there.

"I'll go to the place you suggest first," I tell him.

"I'll meet you there," he says and hangs up.

Blackman is better at this than I am. He has years of investigative work on me, as well as years of studying sick and twisted serial murderers behind him. With Eva's life on the line, I'm not too proud to admit that. He deduced the location of Sleeping Beauty on nothing but sparse evidence, an incomplete profile, and experience. I should listen to his advice.

30

EVA

A row of broken springs in the thin mattress is poking me in a spot just above my lower back, growing more and more painful. The little I can move due to the tight restraints I'm in does nothing to relieve it.

The fog in my brain caused by whatever he's giving me to sedate me is receding, waking other aches and pain associated with lying in the same position all the time.

Whatever he gives me makes it hard to want anything but to sleep and rest. Makes it hard to care about anything other than that.

But as it fades, everything returns.

My heart's racing, flushing the drugs out of my body even faster, and I'm struggling to get out of my restraints so hard the whole bed is rattling. I'm not tied down with ropes, but chains. I can hear them clinking against the metal bed frame.

And I'm wearing a diaper. The indignity as I realize it needs to be changed brings angry tears to my eyes.

I don't remember him ever changing it, which is a blessing, though just imagining it happening is bad in itself.

He's late coming to renew my dose of the sedative.

And the implications of that are a frenzy of fear, sadness, and anxiety in my brain, culminating in utter terror. I'll starve to death in this bed, I'll die covered in my own shit, he's letting my mind get clear so I'll feel every last thing he plans to do to me. The cycle just goes on and on and no amount of deep breathing and telling myself to calm down is helping. It's like all the emotions of this ordeal I didn't feel because I was drugged out of my mind are coming back all at once, jumbled together, no head or tail to them.

The room is freezing cold, so cold I'm shivering, and the draft from the broken window is growing colder. It's bringing in the clean, pure scent of fresh, undisturbed snow and nothing else.

The house is creaking around me, wood settling, pipes clanking, air hissing in radiators that don't work.

And footsteps. Coming closer. Falling against the floorboards in the hallway, softly and steadily, but I hear it as a stampede of wild animals.

I'm about to find out what Selima went through, what all the victims of The Fairytale Killer went through. It would make one hell of an article. One I'll never write.

A door creaks open.

Worrying about what will happen is not worse than finding out for certain.

I scream. It's the last thing I can still do to save myself. My last goodbye.

31

MARK

The bright white spots that are the four farms we're looking at are pulsing on the screen like living things as I walk back to Schmitt. I'm trying not to imagine Eva alone in one of the cold rooms of those houses. But it's better than imagining her dead.

"That one seems most likely," I say and point to the one Blackman suggested. It's in the lower-left corner of the big screen. "But I want to check them all."

"The tactical unit told me we don't have the manpower to check them all at the same time," Schmitt says. "at least not thoroughly. Maybe two, they're saying, if they stretch themselves thin. Perhaps it's best we check one at a time."

The blue-green light of the screen is reflected on his hard as stone, expressionless face, making his dark eyes glow unnaturally.

"There's not enough time," I say, the words hurting my throat and mouth since they come out like broken glass.

A flash in his eyes tells me he already thinks it's too late. He doesn't say it though.

"So that one," Schmitt says. "I'll make the calls."

He leaves to make the arrangements, and the longer I look at the pulsing screen the more unbearable the tightness and nausea in my stomach grow. This is my last chance—my only chance—to save Eva. And my intuition, or gut, or whatever you want to call it is telling me to check the apple farm too.

The problem is, I dare not trust it.

What Blackman said all makes perfect sense. It's close to the main road, hidden by a copse of pine trees, and it was a cattle farm just fifteen years ago. The facilities for the kind of work The Fairytale Killer does are all there and fully equipped.

And what do I have to go on? The fact that Snow White took a bite of a poisoned apple?

It's not enough.

"Tactical will need an hour to prepare," Schmitt informs me in a gruff voice.

"Maybe you should just hit it with all you've got, all at once," I suggest. "It is the most likely place and the biggest. Trying to go in stealthily will just take too much time. That way tactical can check the other two larger farms."

His first reaction is pity and disbelief, but I don't break eye contact with him as he considers my suggestion. It takes a couple of seconds, but eventually, he nods, his eyes narrowing as he thinks.

"You make a good point, Novak," he says.

"And I'm going to the apple place," I say before even fully deciding to.

The longer I think about it, the more it's nagging at me that I need to check the place. I've learned to trust my flashes of intuition over the years. They're a hard thing to pin down, and even harder to explain, but ignoring them never brings anything good. It always just takes me on a longer, more round-about way to the thing I should've done in the first place. But too much is riding on the outcome of this operation to tie all the forces we have at our disposal to my gut feeling.

"What? Alone?" Schmitt asks.

"I'll call if I need backup," I say. "Don't worry, I have the training."

I don't know if it's the worst idea I've ever had or the best one. I just know I can't sit around and wait any longer. If they find her at the slaughterhouse, then they'll find her. If they don't, we've put all our eggs in one basket and lost. I won't be able to live with myself if that happens. I might not be able to live with myself if we find Eva dead, but I'll worry about that after, not before. Not now.

I'm good at reading maps. It actually has nothing to do with being in the Army and everything to do with my grandfather's love of hiking. He was happiest on the trail, and we used to take these long multi-day hikes in the wilderness together. He started taking me along as soon as I was old enough to walk without falling every ten steps, as he put it. I've almost forgiven myself for not going with him on his last hike, the one on which his heart stopped. We argued, and I refused to go with him. I was sixteen and stupid. Might be I could've saved him. I try not to think about it too much and this is certainly not the time for it.

I mapped out the best approach to the orchard on the hour-long drive to the farm, which only took me a little over forty-five minutes.

Now I'm standing under tall, lance straight pine trees that were planted around the property to protect the orchards from the worst of the north wind. Said wind is strong tonight, frost laden, cold and cutting as a razor blade. But it's driving the clouds away, so the night is clear thanks to it. I'm waiting for my eyes to adjust to the darkness. The moon is half full but hanging high in the sky, its silvery-white light reflecting off the snow covering the field, casting more than enough light to see by.

Before me, there's a vast field dotted with spindly, gnarled, bent, broken, and fallen apple trees. The fastest way to the farm buildings is across it. I can just barely make them out as denser, darker blobs against the night sky in the distance. The stealthier way to approach is longer, under the tall pines that surround the property. Despite my need to get to the building as fast as I can, I choose that one.

There's not much snow under the pines, and my footsteps are muffled by the blanket of fallen needles and the hissing and creaking of the trees.

I can make out more and more of the farm buildings the closer I get. There's a large, boxy, three-story house dominating the side where I'm approaching from, blocking my view of the rest of the structures. It has small windows, five a floor, all identical, and all dark. If I didn't know better, I'd say it was a dorm of some sort or a nursing home. But it's most likely a family home from a long time ago, when this type of simple construction was the way to go for building affordable, large family homes.

The line of pines ends about two-hundred meters before the buildings. I will have to cross that open ground and climb over a wooden fence surrounding the complex and do it all in plain view of all those windows. At least I'm wearing a dark coat and dark pants.

Just as I'm about to make a run for it the sounds of a car engine overpowers the hissing of the pines. A car is approaching up the winding road leading to the entrance, its glowing orange lights shining through the line of pine trees opposite me.

I don't think, just run to intercept the car before it reaches the farm. Whoever's in it, even if it's the owner coming to check on his property, will answer my questions before he does anything tonight.

But I know this isn't just an innocent visit.

This is the killer returning to his lair. If I allowed myself to think of anything other than getting in position to intercept him, I'd be hoping he's here to start his work and not finish it. But I'm not thinking. I'm just letting my training guide my footsteps, glad I kept up with it.

I reach the shadowy area around the big house just as the car pulls into the courtyard. I pull my gun from the pocket of my coat. I don't carry it daily, just keep it in the glove box of my car, and I didn't want to waste time putting on the holster before coming here. Good thing too, otherwise I'd have missed this guy by moments.

I jog along the house to the corner, no longer mindful of the noise I'm making. The sound of the engine and the crunching gravel under the approaching car's tires are masking any noise I'm making anyway.

The car's headlights are illuminating the larger face of the house, revealing large, ornate double doors and the tall windows on that side. Thankfully, the beam is missing the corner of the house where I'm hiding, keeping me hidden in the darkness.

The driver makes a U-turn in the courtyard, coming to a stop with the back of the car facing the front door and the front exit from the compound.

He turns off the engine, the lights going out at the same time. Looking at glaring headlights has destroyed my night vision.

The driver opens his door, which is now on the other side of the car from where I'm standing and gets out slowly. He's wearing a long coat with the collar popped and a brimmed hat. I can't see his face at all, and I give it a few seconds to see if there's anyone else in the car. He makes his way towards the door, walking slowly and carefully since it's very dark and most likely icy.

No one else gets out of the black or dark blue Kia sedan he drove here in.

"Stop or I shoot!" I say in my most menacingly commanding voice.

The man flinches, but doesn't turn to me. Instead, he shuffles back to the car, which is more than fifty meters away from where I'm hiding.

I hesitate before making good on my threat, giving him enough time to get inside the car. Stupid. By the time I fire the first shot, aiming at the tires, the engine is already on.

He speeds off and I run after him, firing off three more shots, but I'm slipping and sliding so badly on the icy ground, they all go wide of the car.

I should've shot first and asked questions later.

The front door of the big house is shut tight but unlocked, and it opens with surprisingly silent ease. The windowless foyer is a wide cavernous room, its edges lost in complete darkness. The moonlight from outside only reaches about a foot into the room, but I can see the outline of a grand wooden staircase in front of me. The house smells of dust, rot, mildew, and something much more sinister. Old blood.

I no longer have any doubt that I found The Fairytale Killer's lair, and that I just missed my best chance of taking him out, but I won't think of that yet. I turn on the flashlight on my phone, thanking whatever genius came up with the idea to install that feature onto these new smart gadgets, and run up the wide staircase, kicking up even more dust and making the smell of rot worse.

The man might be back at any moment and he has a much better knowledge of this building and its secrets than I do. The wide stairs separate the first floor into two identical hallways, lined with identical dark wood doors, all of which are shut. The floor's been swept, but not neatly and a set of faint footprints —made by boots with a rugged sole good for walking on snow and ice—are leading down the one on the left-hand side.

As good a place as any to start, so I follow them.

I'm halfway down the hall when a faint, desperate scream sounds from further down the hall. It's more a cry than a scream and tugs at something so deep inside me I don't think, I just sprint towards it.

She screams louder as I kick the door to the room open.

"Eva! It's me," I tell her, cutting her off mid-scream, or mid-wail, more like.

I'll never forget the terrible sound of her cry for help, but I already know I'll forever hope to.

"Mark?" she whispers like she doesn't believe it. I shine the flashlight at the wall by the door and find the light switch. It's an old circular switch, with a smaller circle in the center to turn the light on, but thankfully it works. The yellow light cast by the bare, dirty bulb in the center of the ceiling shows me a scene from my worst nightmare. But at least Eva's alive. At least I found her in time.

"Yes, it's me, I found you, are you OK?" I'm rambling as I rush to her bedside. She's lying on a metal camp bed with a thin red and blue-striped mattress. That and the wooden chair next to it are the only two pieces of furniture in this cavernous room with four tiny windows.

Her wrists and her ankles are secured to the frame of the bed with the kind of padded restraints they use in hospitals so patients don't hurt themselves and a wide, dark blindfold is covering her bright blue eyes. My hands start shaking as I fumble to undo the restraints, but I will them to stop and they do. This is no time to lose it. I still have to get her out of here, we're not safe yet. Why the fuck did I come here alone?

Her hair is dyed black and cut shorter than it was. She's only wearing a thin, sleeveless white nightshirt, the lace collar cinched tight around her neck.

Her legs and her arms are ice cold and she's shivering so hard her teeth are chattering. She's trying to speak but can't.

"It's all right, you're safe now, you're all right, I'm here," I say as I struggle to take off my coat without letting go of her. I finally manage to wrap it around her.

I'm lying to her. We're not safe. The psycho could be back at any minute and if Eva isn't suffering from hypothermia from lying motionless in this freezing cold room, she will be by the time I get her to my car, which I left almost a kilometer away from here.

I hold her tight with one arm and reach for my phone, guided to it by the flashlight that's still on. It's hard holding onto her while keeping the gun pointed at the darkness beyond the door and dialing Schmitt's number at the same time, but I do it.

It rings for so long I'm beginning to give up on him by the time he finally answers.

Luckily, he's a sharp and clever man. He quickly makes sense of what I'm telling him and promises he'll come here with reinforcements right away.

Eva is holding me around the neck as hard as she can, which isn't very hard at all. She's still shaking very hard.

"It was a young man, heavily tattooed. I would recognize him again if I saw him," she whispers, breathing hard. I can feel the effort it's taking her to tell me all this. "But there's another one. An older one with a very clear voice. Hearing him speak was like listening to someone read. His German was perfect. Too perfect. No accent I could hear."

I caress her hair even as I hold her closer. Her shivering's getting worse, not better. "That's excellent information, Eva. You did really well, you're so strong. They've arrested the young man. We're still looking for the older one, but we'll find him. You're safe now. You can rest. You'll tell me everything once you're recovered. I'm sure it'll be a lot of help."

She shivers violently and whimpers, trying to hold me tighter but not succeeding. I hate what he's done to her. He's reduced my strong, independent Eva to this shivering, whimpering, weak woman.

It's my fault she's here. My fault, because I couldn't track down the psycho fast enough, because I believed she was ignoring my calls instead of knowing something was wrong. I could've started looking for her days ago. And then maybe her nightmare would be less horrible.

Her hair smells of hair dye, the harsh chemical scent making my nose itch. I wish I could offer her more than my arms around her and my coat. I wish I could give her these days she spent here back. And I wish I'd shot the bastard when I had the chance. I'll have to live with these failures for the rest of my life. I know it like I know that all I've done has not been enough.

32

MARK

The night sky outside the fifth-floor hospital room is still pitch dark, even darker than it was because the moon has long since set. Eva is sleeping peacefully in a bed that looks too big for her slight frame, her unnaturally black hair a stark contrast against the pristine white of the pillow. Her face is as pale as the sheets, her lips still tinged blue.

They messed up when they brought her in, gave her some type of sedative that mixed badly with whatever her captor was giving her—Valerian most likely—and made her worse before she started getting better. But the arrhythmia it caused seems to be fine now. She's connected to a monitor that's recording her vitals and her heartbeat is finally returning to a normal, healthy rhythm. It kept fluctuating all night, kept forming a completely wrong kind of green glowing line on the monitor, jagged and irregular, and kept scaring me to death.

Schmitt and his officers came as quickly as he promised they would. They saw no black or dark blue Kia sedan on their approach, but they did find the seven dwarfs. Underfed and on the edge of hypothermia, so heavily sedated and malnourished that they're still fighting to keep two of them alive, but on the whole, it's the best outcome that any of us could've hoped for.

They're still searching the house, but they've already recovered so much evidence that they hardly need any more. Fingerprints, DNA, fibers, the superglue, buckets of blood. There's no doubt that we've discovered the place where The Fairytale Killer's killed his victims, and there's no doubt he wasn't careful at all while he was there.

All we have to do now is find the man himself.

Just like before.

I should've shot the bastard when I had the chance.

I haven't left Eva's side since they brought her here. Others are looking for the car and the man I saw. Others are sifting through the evidence. I'm terrified that the psycho will come here and try to finish what he started with Eva. A man so concerned with making everything perfect will not leave loose ends. Six German police officers are guarding her here, but I trust no one but myself to keep her safe. Like I should've done from the start. Like I failed to do.

THE FAIRYTALE KILLER

The piercing sound of an ambulance siren wakes me with a jolt. It takes me a second to see clearly, to know where I am. The hospital, Eva's safe, we stopped him.

Schmitt is standing over Eva's bed looking at her sleeping.

I lunge to my feet, grunting at him to get away from her.

It's him. How could it not be? I knew it all along.

Then he looks at me, his piercing, black eyes friendly, concerned even.

"They tell me she is going to be fine," he says. "I'm sorry I woke you."

I sit back down and rub my eyes with the thumb and forefinger of my right hand, my palm snagging against the beginnings of a beard. When I open my eyes again I notice the light in the room is coming from outside. It's the end of a clear, sunny day, the setting sun coloring the blue sky a pale yellow in the west.

"I slept all day, didn't I?" I say, more to myself than him. The dull pain in my lower back and the sharp one in my neck are screaming, Yes! to that question.

"You needed to so we let you," Schmitt says. He's still wearing his dark blue coat, and it's buttoned up to the neck. His cheeks are red with windburn. The brilliant blue sky and yellow sun were a lie. It must've been a freezing cold day today.

"We could use your help now," he adds and holds out the tan envelope he's holding. It's sealed with all sorts of things, including a black, red, and yellow string that the Germans use to seal their most important documents. I look at it, then back up at him, not taking it.

"This is all the fingerprint and DNA evidence we've recovered so far," he says. "I am officially requesting your help in processing it. And giving you the chance to determine if this was the work of one of yours."

I fix my hair back with both hands and take the envelope.

"Deliver it to your lab yourself, please," he says. "But you might want to go home to shower and change first."

He's got a very good point.

"I have people I trust that can come and collect this," I say. "I'm not leaving Eva alone. He might come back for her."

Schmitt exhales sharply. "There are six officers just on this floor and more in the lobby and outside. I was carded three times before they let me in here and they all know me. We're leaving nothing to chance. You can trust us."

"And I do," I say, not standing up.

He shrugs. "Call me when you find anything out, and I'll do the same."

I promise I will and he leaves.

I should get back to work.

But Eva's still as pale as the sheets and I can't bear even the thought of leaving her, let alone trying to do it.

There's only about five percent of battery left on my phone as I call Sargent Ross to come and collect the evidence. He's full of questions, but I keep the conversation brief.

Eva's blinking at me when I hang up and look at her again.

"I'm sorry I woke you," I tell her softly. Her eyes are as bright blue as the pristine sky outside.

"I have to tell you. That man who abducted me, the young muscular one, the same one Selima dated, I'm sure…" she pauses to take a shuddering breath. "His name is Russell Parcivall, with a weird spelling, two Ls. And his father, Wallace Parcivall, he's a US Army man, he might be the old man, who… who…who…"

She can't say it, and I don't want her to try.

I take her hand and stroke her hair. "When did you find all this out?"

"Right before the guy abducted me…someone sent me a link to an article about him…I was going to tell you at dinner," she says, her voice growing fainter and fainter. The effects of the medicine screw-up are still lingering. Or maybe this is just the aftermath of the shock she's had.

"I know about Russell," I tell her, since I know apologizing for not meeting her for dinner that night, which is what I really want to do, won't change a damn thing. "But Wallace, he's been dead for a while now."

Her eyes get even wider. "Who then?"

I shrug. "They'll find whoever it is."

"They?" she asks, her eyes narrowing in that sharp, questioning way that's her signature look. "Not you?"

I pull up a chair and sit down next to her bed, not letting go of her hand. "I'm going to stay right here until you recover. I'm not letting you out of my sight again."

She squeezes my hand, her eyes turning watery, but then they harden. "Mark, no. I will be fine. I'm a big girl and you have a job to do."

The strength with which she says it almost makes me believe it.

"I'd prefer to stay right here," I say with a smile. "They've got two hundred people working on this case. They don't need me."

"I need you to find this psycho," she says, putting so much force into it her heart rate rises high enough to cause the monitor she's attached to start beeping shrilly.

Her eyes are huge and full of determination. There's no arguing with her when she looks at me like this, I know it from past experience. She'll have her way in this. And I dare to let in just a sliver of hope that I'll have her back soon. Complete and unharmed. Safe and whole.

Blackman is standing at the nurses' station in the lobby, surrounded by two officers. He's trying to explain who he is and why he needs to get to Eva's room. He's not calling it that, he's calling it the witness' room, but he's got no official ID to show them, so the officers aren't budging.

I walk over and show them my ID. One of the officers is Hans, the young man who drove me to the Snow White murder scene what feels like years ago, but was really less than a week ago.

He nods and stands aside so I can face Blackman.

"What are you doing here?" I ask him.

"Novak, good," he says. "I spoke to Sargent Ross, and he told me you sent him to pick something up from the hospital. Since my hotel is just around the corner from here and I was on my way to the base, I told him I can pick it up. But they won't let me go up."

He's flustered and agitated and talking too loudly. I show him the evidence bag I'm holding. "I have it here," I tell him. "I was just heading to the base to bring it in myself. We can go together."

His lips are moving like he's about to start talking, but he doesn't.

"Come on," I say. "We'll have to take a taxi. Unless you have a car?"

He looks at me sharply, then shakes his head. "No, I don't have a car."

I point at the revolving doors and let him precede me out into the blistering cold. The sun has set and the brilliant blue sky is turning dark fast.

There's a line of taxis along the curb to the left of the hospital entrance. I walk to the first one, making sure Blackman is following. I open the back door and let him get in first, before taking a seat beside him.

The interior smells of leather and a cloying artificial pine car freshener. I tell the driver where to go, then lean back in my seat and close my eyes like I'm about to doze off. But I don't think I've ever been more awake. I need to finish this, or neither Eva nor I will ever have any peace.

33

MARK

There's a flurry of activity around the HQ building at the base, as there usually is around this time of the evening. People finishing their workday, going to dinner or out for the evening. I tell the taxi driver to let us out in front of the gates to the base. It's a short, less than five-minute walk to HQ from there and I suggest it to Blackman under the pretense of needing some fresh air and to stretch my legs. It's not really a pretense. I do need both those things, but I can get plenty once the black cloud of this case is no longer hanging over my head.

"What made you decide to go to that apple farm instead of the slaughterhouse?" Blackman asks as we're walking. He's pulled the collar of his long dark coat high around his neck and is holding it closed.

"It was a spur-of-the-moment decision, more intuition than logical thinking," I say, telling him the truth. "And it's a good thing I did. I got a good look at the man who came there to finish what he started. And his car."

That part's a lie.

He looks sideways at me, only his eyes and nose visible above the collar of his coat. His breath is a perpetual cloud of white mist.

"The German police are scouring the area for him," I say. "And I stayed at the hospital all night in case he decided to come and finish what he started with Eva. He's not the type to leave loose ends, now is he?"

We've reached the HQ building and I hold open the door for him to enter first.

"He didn't?" Blackman asks.

I shake my head and shrug. "I still hope he might."

"And the man you arrested yesterday, has he said anything?" Blackman asks. "I had a suspicion that we were looking for more than one person."

He never mentioned that suspicion to me. But I don't say that.

"His injuries are still being tended," I say, pressing the button to call the elevator. "The Russians did quite a number on him. They think he might lose his whole left hand."

Blackman's face shows no reaction. None at all. He's so pale his skin has taken on a bluish tone.

"But he got off easy, even if he does," I add, just as the elevator arrives. "Frankly, I'm surprised the Russians didn't kill him outright."

"Why…why do you think they didn't?" he asks.

"I think he told them he wasn't working alone, the same as he told me," I say and let him precede me out of the elevator. "or maybe he was in so much pain he just wanted his daddy."

That did it. He turns to me sharply, his face still a pale bluish mask, but his eyes alight.

"Why do you mock him?" he snaps. "There's nothing funny about any of this. Your girlfriend almost died, didn't she? What's there to laugh about?"

He's displaying all the aggressive frustration of an old man too set in his ways to allow for any more change.

"He wants to be taken seriously. Both he and his father do," I say with a shrug as I use my keycard to unlock the metal doors leading to the lab. "But they're just a couple of deranged psychos. And I won't take that seriously. I'll just make sure they never see the light of day again."

"Wallace Parcivall was a psycho," Blackman mutters as we enter the lab proper. "He was never punished for it."

"I know letting him go must've been a blow to you," I say as I lead the way to the office he appropriated for his use. The Top Secret file on Wallace is lying open in the middle of the desk atop the photos and reports from the crime scenes. "I'd like to talk more about that case with you. But let me first have a word with Sargent Ross."

I leave him there and shut the door behind me. Ross

is already standing by the table in the middle of the room.

"I was going to get the evidence from you at the hospital, Sir," he says. "But then Blackman said—"

"Follow me, Sargent," I say, interrupting him as I stride to the metal door that leads to the labs.

Once the door closes behind us, I lead him further into one of the empty offices.

"I need you to call some MPs down here and have them guard the entrance to the lab," I tell him. "No one is to leave until I say so."

He's looking at me like I've lost my mind, but swallows hard instead of saying anything of the sort. "We have to protect this evidence," I add to make it easier for him.

"Yes, Sir," he finally says.

"But first, get Wanda and tell her to come in here."

He leaves with another, "Yes, Sir." And a couple of minutes later, Wanda comes in on his heels. I hand her the evidence folder Schmitt left for me.

"I'd like you to first process the fingerprint evidence from the victim's room. You'll find them in the folder. They should be clearly labeled," I say. "Run them against everyone working here. Starting with me. And Blackman. Then check it against all the fingerprints we have, including the one on the photo."

"You want me to run them through the database of our personnel first?" she asks.

Now both she and Ross are looking at me like I'm not making much sense. Or making the kind of sense they'd rather never hear from me again. I got us all in trouble after the first two victims were found, by having them check things that I had no permission to be checking.

"This is on my authority," I tell them. "How long will it take?"

Wanda glances at Ross who doesn't return her look.

"Not long, an hour maybe," she tells me.

"Get it done," I say to her and leave.

If I'm right, we'll know the identity of The Fairytale Killer in an hour or less. If I'm wrong, I very well might get that dishonorable discharge I so narrowly escaped a few months ago.

After leaving Wanda and Ross I stayed in the empty office and made a call to Thompson to appraise him of the situation and find out a few things I still need to know. He sounded tired as he answered my questions and didn't have any of his own.

Blackman is sitting with his back to the windows of the office. He's taken off his coat, but didn't hang it up. Instead, he's laid it over his lap and is clutching it like a blanket in his white-knuckled hands.

He's staring at Parcivall's file, at the photo of the Parcivall family, more precisely, and he didn't stir as I walked in and shut the door. The girl in the photo has such a vacant, faraway look in her eyes she looks more like a doll than a person, and the boy's—Russell's—face looks angry, rageful to the point of insanity. Their father, Wallace is sporting a big bushy mustache, his lips curled upwards underneath it. But his eyes aren't smiling.

"Those kids went through a lot, didn't they?" I ask as I take off my coat, lay it over a chair, and sit down opposite him.

"They didn't deserve what they got," Blackman says. "None of it. And what rankles the most is that they could've been saved if the Military had only acted on my findings and removed the children from him in time. But instead, they let that monster continue torturing them in the interests of National Security. Well now they have an international incident on their hands, don't they? This will make the US Military even less popular than it already is, and I can't say I'm sorry."

I pull the file towards me and flip it over, then start leafing through it. Much of it is redacted, whole passages crossed out with thick black lines. Especially the documents dealing with the investigation Blackman conducted.

"That must've been hard," I say. "Keeping silent all these years, I mean. And watching Wallace rise the way he did, despite all the damage he'd done."

He looks at me, his light eyes watery yet gleaming like the noon sun reflecting off clear water. Sharp. But I think it's the first honest look he's given me since we met.

"I've never had a case where I had to watch a guilty

man walk free," I say. "And I know I couldn't stand it. I'd resign the day it happened."

"I stayed on for a while," he says. "Hoping justice will prevail. It didn't."

"So you made your own justice," I say and leave it at that, returning his honest look, keeping mine such as best I can.

He inclines his head at me and grins, then looks down at the photos of the victims.

"Rebecca was a true innocent. Still more a young girl than a young woman when she died," he said. "Her doctors thought she disassociated completely at the age of ten. She never grew past that age psychologically."

This case sucked me in deep from the start and almost took me under completely when Eva was taken. What would I have done if one of the bodies I'd been called to examine was her? Would I ever surface from the depths of that insanity?

I'll never have to find out. But I don't think the answer to that question is yes.

"She loved those princess cartoons," he mutters, more to himself than me. I purposefully kept the file open at the family photo and he's looking at it now, his eyes just watery now. "They were her escape. Pocahontas was her favorite. She loved how Pocahontas took the name Rebecca as her Christian name. She hated Beauty and the Beast because Beast terrified her."

"You made sure she got the help she needed, didn't you?" I ask. "After you left the military and your hands were free to help the children as a civilian."

I'm guessing here, since I didn't have the time to confirm this suspicion yet. But I don't think I'm wrong.

Gleaming light flashes across Blackman's eyes again. "It was too late. I was too late to save her."

"So you decided to avenge her by killing the princesses she loved," I say with too much venom in my voice. I'm supposed to be keeping this friendly, coaxing the information out of him as if I care and understand him.

His grin twists into a grimace. I'm ready for him to deny it, I know it's coming, I don't want to hear it. Whether I get his confession or not, I'm sure he left us overwhelming evidence at that farm. Eva would most likely be able to recognize his voice too. But I want to hear him admit the monstrous crimes he's committed.

"They were masterpieces though," I say, hoping I'm right about the part of my profile of the killer where I assumed he's high on the narcissism spectrum. "Not just the scenes themselves, which were perfect, but everything else too. You planted just enough evidence to make us feel like we were doing something and getting somewhere, while the whole time our wheels were just spinning in the mud you created, so to speak."

He likes the praise, I can see it in his arrogant, self-satisfied grin and the way his eyes are now gleaming with liquid light. Dangerous.

I should stroke his ego some more. Then he'll tell me more. But doing it is making me nauseous and bringing back my migraine headache. The deeper I go into his reasons, his insanity, the more I just want to get as far away from him as I can. Early on in this case, I knew we were looking for a madman, a person so outside the sphere of normality he's in a circle of his own. I knew talking to the man as a human being would be hard. It's proving damn near impossible.

"You left us the witnesses to find too, didn't you?" I ask. "That was masterful. The kid in the teahouse and the prostitute. You made sure she had the name too, didn't you? Are you were the one sending Eva the photos and the articles, weren't you?"

"But she didn't check them in time," he blurts out, his eyes locking on mine, only a ring of pale blue color left around the black of his dilated pupils. He sighs and takes the photo of the Parcivall family in his hands, holding it so his thumb covers the father's face.

"He killed their mother, you know," he says. "Pushed her down the stairs in front of them. Let her lie there dying in her own blood while he got them ready for school. That night, after the cops investigated and cleared the scene, he made them scrub her blood off the floor. They worked all night. Rebecca was five, Russell seven. Neither of them recovered. Rebecca retreated into a fantasy world inside her head and she never quite left it after that. But the boy, he shot his father a few years later. Unfortunately, he missed anything vital, so the father was back home with them in two weeks. That's when I was brought in to investigate and I found everything out. I had two weeks to stop him returning, but I failed. And I couldn't even keep them away from him. Your reporter girlfriend was supposed to tell you all this days ago, but she's slow and lazy."

I have no idea where I'm getting the strength not to fly over the table at him and choke him until his eyes are as dead as Eva's almost were.

"But even if she had, she'd still end up as Snow White," he concludes. "That I decided as soon as I saw you two together. What better way to get the publicity and attention I needed than to make the investigator's woman one of my victims?"

It's not a question he wants to be answered and I couldn't if I wanted it. My jaw is clenched together too tight as I struggle not to say what I really mean and do what I really want to do. It'll do me no good to kill him now. I had my one and only chance last night and I missed it.

"I took no pleasure in the killings, you understand," he says. "But they had to be done and they had to be done perfectly. Russell and I, we got our revenge for Rebecca, and for all the years the children suffered. It's not my fault. It is the unjust, unfair system that rewards monsters and has the ability and the will to shelter them that's to blame."

Outside the office, Thompson is standing by the large interactive table, flanked by two MPs. Wanda and Ross are there too, off to the side, Wanda clutching a stack of papers so hard she's crinkling them.

"I believe that you took no pleasure in the killings," I say and that's no lie. There was no passion in the murders. Only clinical, methodical precision as though the killer was just doing a thing that needed to be done. So many lives lost to prove a point. So many people terrified by deeds that will forever remain incomprehensible. Two wrongs will never make a right, no matter how you twist and turn them. "But you were beginning to enjoy them, weren't you? Hence the repeats of princesses you'd already killed?"

"I knew you were a worthy adversary," he says, inclining his head at me. "It could be you sitting where I'm sitting."

That cuts deep, but I don't let it show on my face. I take one last look into his eyes, at all the vast, watery nothingness in them, and then I'm done. I won't glorify what he did by listening to another minute of his rationalizations.

I walk out and leave the office door open.

"You can take him now," I say to Thompson. "He's confessed to being The Fairytale Killer. I'll have my report ready in an hour. Then you can do with him as you see fit."

Thompson nods but remains silent. He looks like he's aged twenty years since I've seen him last.

"He was my friend since we were teenagers," he says quietly. "What do I do with him?"

I will not even try to answer that. I don't think he wants me to.

"In the end, he used you to get close to this investigation," I say. "I believe your friend, the man you knew has not been around for fifteen years or more."

Thompson nods again. "I expect you're right."

He tells the MPs to take Blackman into custody and I stand off to the side as they do. Blackman's eyes are almost as blank as Rebecca Parcivall's were in that photo, but the defiant grin on his face as he passes first me, then Thompson as though I'm not there tells me he believes he has won. And in a lot of ways, he has.

34

EVA

Upbeat music is blaring in my headphones, a happy song, one you can dance to. I keep it so loud they can probably hear it next door, although I'm using headphones. Maybe I'm wrong. It's not bothering Mark one bit, he's fast asleep in my bed—our bed now that it's all over.

Only it's not over. Not yet.

I never used to be able to write to music, but now I can't stand the silence. Chained to that bed with nothing but silence and fuzzy dreams for company has destroyed my love of both.

Outside, tiny little snowflakes are falling, but I bet they'll grow thicker soon. Before the street lamps all went out at one AM, the night had an eerie, dark orange glow. Now it's just black.

The ice flower in the corner of my living room

window is there again, gorgeous and big, but it doesn't interest me anymore. Nothing much does anymore.

I'm happiest working. Writing. Keeping busy.

The woman who escaped a serial killer. The most notorious serial killer the world has ever seen. My story is in high demand.

The Fairytale Killer—Otto Blackman, retired Colonel of the United States Army, who killed to avenge a wrong done to a girl he couldn't save.

I've stopped apologizing to Mark for not wanting to do any of the things we used to do. He still hasn't stopped apologizing for not catching the killer before I was harmed. Each morning he wakes up and I'm not in bed beside him, the apologizing cycle starts all over again. It's not his fault. He did what he could. He did more than enough. He doesn't believe me when I tell him that, but I won't stop until he does.

They wanted to keep me in the hospital for a week, but I checked myself out after three days. As soon as I could walk, I couldn't stay in bed anymore, I'd pace the room until I was too tired to stand then fall asleep in a chair. That was four weeks ago. I still can't sleep in a bed. And I can't sleep in darkness, so I sleep during the day on the sofa.

I need the space, the peace, the ability to do only what I want to do, and nothing else. Mark understands, I know he does. Deep down underneath all the self-blame and self-reproach, he wants the same thing. We'll find our way back to the easy love we used to share.

Otto Blackman sent his manifesto to all the news outlets he could find, revealing his reasons for what he did in minute detail. The man who helped him, Russell Parcivall, is currently held on the closed ward of the hospital for the criminally insane.

I've started writing a book about what they did and why.

Blackman has agreed to let me interview him.

Mark is waving at me from the kitchen doorway, his hair a mess, his eyes still half-closed. He's wearing a white t-shirt and dark blue pajama bottoms, both well-worn. Like always, just the sight of him fills me with a sharp, deep longing for simple things, a simple life, lazy days spent well. Longing for what we used to have when days passed fast like hours when we were together.

I take off my headphones, the song spilling into the room nearly as loudly as it was spilling into my ears a second ago.

"Did the music wake you?" I ask, closing the lid of my laptop to make it stop playing and setting it all on the coffee table. "I'm sorry."

"You're not coming to bed?" he asks. "It's past four AM."

When he went to bed at midnight, I promised I'd be right there. I didn't lie. Not exactly.

I walk over to him, pulled like a magnet to the peace and joy his presence, his look, his arms around me used to wake in me. Joy and peace and love I had given up trying to find in another person by the time I met him.

I reach out my hands and he takes them, pulling me into a loose embrace.

"I have to prepare for the interview," I say.

He winces, his arms growing tense. "Are you sure you want to speak to him?"

He's been asking me that since Blackman agreed to grant me an exclusive interview.

"He just wants the publicity," Mark adds. "He's a very sick man, Eva, even if the German psychologists deemed him fit to stand trial."

He's said this before too. Many times. And I could tell him what I've already told him many times. That I'm a grown woman and I can handle speaking to that man. That whatever Blackman was, he was also one of the leading forensic psychologists in the world and his specialty was serial killers. The fact that he then turned into a serial killer is big news echoing across the world. I've already gotten a huge advance on the book I'm writing about him and what he put me through. More money than I usually make in a year.

"I don't want to argue about this anymore, Mark," I tell him. I just want him to hold me and remind me of how it used to be, let me remember only the good times.

"Yeah, me neither," he says and pulls me into a tighter embrace, stroking my short hair. I shaved off the dyed black hair three days after I left the hospital. I couldn't look in the mirror without remembering the fear and desperation of lying motionless on that disgusting camp bed.

But even that memory isn't as heavy or piercing as it was. Not when Mark's holding me.

"I think I could sleep now," I whisper into his chest where his heart is racing. "Let's go back to bed."

Once I'm laying by his side in the bed, he kept warm for us, my head resting on his chest and his arm around me, I know I didn't lie. I could sleep. I can do anything when we're together. Better than I ever could alone. We'll find our way back to the place where I knew that for certain every minute of every day. I know we will.

MARK

Mere hours after his confession Blackman was handed over to the German authorities and all connections between the US Military, past, present, and future were severed. He will be tried and, hopefully, incarcerated here.

The evidence against him is overwhelming. He was not careful at the abandoned farm where he kept, killed, and prepared his victims. There were several barrels of gasoline in the basement of the house where I found Eva. He was planning to torch it all after the last murder, his coup de grâce, Snow White and the Seven Dwarfs. Only six of the seven dwarfs survived. One of them succumbed to hypothermia three days after we found them.

I'm sitting in a car outside the jailhouse where

they're holding him, waiting for Eva to finish her interview with Blackman. Outside, snow is falling softly and insistently. The windshield is already covered with an inch thick blanket of snow as soft as gauze. I wish I was anywhere but here, even in the room with Blackman and her.

She wants to do this, and she needs to do it alone. She keeps claiming it's because of her book, and gets angry when I suggest she's doing it to find closure, to confront her tormentor. She's sure she's not scarred by it as deeply as I think she is. It was only two days, is her main argument.

I'm afraid she's just buried the fear and terror of it so deep down in her mind, she'll just suffer all over again when it comes gushing back out.

But what do I really know?

Certainly not enough to have caught the guy sooner. Certainly not enough to recognize the most deranged murderer I've ever met or read about when he was standing right next to me.

She wants to talk to Russell Parcivall too, but thankfully, the Germans have locked him up so tight it'll be months before they even consider her request.

It's freezing inside the car, but I like the soft silence the blanket of snow is creating inside the car. It calms me the way few things do anymore.

Eva does.

She's walking towards the car, wrapped in her long parka, a knitted black cap with a huge pouf on her head. Her small pale face is glowing amid all that black, but not as brightly as her eyes. Those are blue as the summer sky and just as vast and welcoming.

I'll never stop blaming myself for failing to uncover Blackman before he could hurt her. My intuition was telling me not to trust him from the moment I first spoke to him, but I didn't listen. And I'll never forget Eva's screams right before I found her. But all of that will fade with time. I'm sure of it. As sure as I am that summer will follow this winter.

THE END

Did you enjoy this story? The next book in this series—Pretty Places (E&M Investigations, Book 1)—is already available!

ALSO BY LJ BOURNE

E&M Investigations Series:

The Fall (Prequel #1)

The Fairytale Killer (Prequel #2)

Pretty Places (E&M Investigations, Book 1)

Bad Roads (E&M Investigations, Book 2)

Lazy Days (E&M Investigations, Book 3)

Ever After (E&M Investigations, Book 4)

Calm Waters (E&M Investigations, Book 5)

You can also...

Join LJ Bourne"s Mailing List to find out more about her books. Sign up by visiting: https://www.lenabourne.com/em-investigations-series-alerts/

ABOUT THE AUTHOR

LJ Bourne is the author of several gripping mystery and crime fiction novels. Her books transport you to vivid, life-like settings where you'll experience heart-pumping action and sinister twists with every turn of the page. With strong, fearless heroines and villains that would make even the toughest detective break a sweat, LJ's books are simply unputdownable.

LJ lives a peaceful life surrounded by her family, cats and koi fish near a tranquil pond by a forest. It's in this idyllic setting that she finds the inspiration to craft her next captivating murder mystery. Though the biggest mystery could actually be why the stories she writes take such dark turns.

Click here to sign up for her newsletter to receive exclusive previews of new books and stay updated on all new releases.

Made in the USA
Coppell, TX
06 March 2024